The Only One

Also from Lauren Blakely

The **Caught Up in Love** Series
(Each book in this series follows a different couple so each book can
be read separately, or enjoyed as a series since characters crossover)
Caught Up in Her (A short prequel novella to *Caught Up in Us*)
Caught Up In Us (A *New York Times* and *USA Today* Bestseller!
Kat and Bryan's romance!)
Pretending He's Mine (A Barnes & Noble and iBooks Bestseller!
Reeve & Sutton's romance!)
Trophy Husband (A *New York Times* and *USA Today* Bestseller!
Chris & McKenna's romance!)
Stars in Their Eyes (An iBooks bestseller!
William and Jess' romance)

Check out my **contemporary romance** novels!
BIG ROCK
Mister O
Well Hung
The Sexy One
Full Package (January 2017)
The Hot One (March 2017)
Joy Stick (Spring 2017)
Far Too Tempting (A *USA Today* bestseller! Matthew and Jane's
romance!)
21 Stolen Kisses (*USA Today* Bestselling forbidden new adult romance!)
Playing With Her Heart (A standalone SEDUCTIVE NIGHTS spin-
off novel about Jill and Davis)

My *USA Today* bestselling
No Regrets series that includes
The Thrill of It
The Start of Us
Every Second With You

The *New York Times* and *USA Today*
Bestselling **Seductive Nights** series including:
First Night (Julia and Clay, prequel novella)
Night After Night (Julia and Clay, book one)
After This Night (Julia and Clay, book two)
One More Night (Julia and Clay, book three)
A Wildly Seductive Night (Julia and Clay novella, book 3.5)
Nights With Him (A standalone novel about Michelle and Jack)
Forbidden Nights (A standalone novel about Nate and Casey)

The **Sinful Nights** Series—the complete New York Times
Bestselling high-heat romantic suspense series that spins off from
Seductive Nights!
Sweet Sinful Nights
Sinful Desire
Sinful Longing
Sinful Love

My *New York Times* and *USA Today*
Bestselling **Fighting Fire** series that includes
Burn For Me (Smith and Jamie)
Melt for Him (Megan and Becker)
Consumed By You (Travis and Cara)

The **Jewel** Series
A two-book sexy contemporary romance series
The Sapphire Affair
The Sapphire Heist

The Only One

A One Love Novella

By Lauren Blakely

1001 Dark Nights

EVIL EYE
CONCEPTS

The Only One
A One Love Novella
By Lauren Blakely

1001 Dark Nights

Published by Evil Eye Concepts, Incorporated

Acknowledgments from the Author

Thank you to Liz and MJ for the amazing opportunity to be part of the Dark Nights family - it is truly a family, and I am grateful and lucky! Thank you to KP Simmon for all the things, and to my editors for making this shine -- Lauren McKellar, Karen Lawson, and more who used their eagle eyes.

Huge gratitude to Dena Marie, who cheered me on and brainstormed every step of the way, and to Jen McCoy, who gave her all, as always.

Thank you to my family and my husband, and to my fabulous dogs! Most of all thanks to the readers.

Xoxo

Lauren

Dedication

This book is dedicated to Dena, who helped find the heart of the story.

Sign up for the 1001 Dark Nights Newsletter
and be entered to win a Tiffany Key necklace.

There's a contest every month!

Go to www.1001DarkNights.com to subscribe.

As a bonus, all subscribers will receive a free
1001 Dark Nights story
The First Night
by Lexi Blake & M.J. Rose

One Thousand and One Dark Nights

Once upon a time, in the future…

*I was a student fascinated with stories and learning.
I studied philosophy, poetry, history, the occult, and
the art and science of love and magic. I had a vast
library at my father's home and collected thousands
of volumes of fantastic tales.*

*I learned all about ancient races and bygone
times. About myths and legends and dreams of all
people through the millennium. And the more I read
the stronger my imagination grew until I discovered
that I was able to travel into the stories... to actually
become part of them.*

*I wish I could say that I listened to my teacher
and respected my gift, as I ought to have. If I had, I
would not be telling you this tale now.
But I was foolhardy and confused, showing off
with bravery.*

*One afternoon, curious about the myth of the
Arabian Nights, I traveled back to ancient Persia to
see for myself if it was true that every day Shahryar
(Persian: شهريار, "king") married a new virgin, and then
sent yesterday's wife to be beheaded. It was written
and I had read, that by the time he met Scheherazade,
the vizier's daughter, he'd killed one thousand
women.*

*Something went wrong with my efforts. I arrived
in the midst of the story and somehow exchanged
places with Scheherazade – a phenomena that had
never occurred before and that still to this day, I
cannot explain.*

*Now I am trapped in that ancient past. I have
taken on Scheherazade's life and the only way I can
protect myself and stay alive is to do what she did to
protect herself and stay alive.*

*Every night the King calls for me and listens as I spin tales.
And when the evening ends and dawn breaks, I stop at a
point that leaves him breathless and yearning for more.
And so the King spares my life for one more day, so that
he might hear the rest of my dark tale.*

*As soon as I finish a story... I begin a new
one... like the one that you, dear reader, have before
you now.*

Prologue

Penny

Ten years ago

The clock mocks me.

As the minute hand ticks closer to eight in the evening, I wrack my brain to figure out if I got the time wrong. Maybe we picked two. Maybe he said ten. Maybe we're meeting tomorrow. My chest twists with a desperate anxiety as I toy with the band on my watch.

But as the fountains of Lincoln Center dance higher under the waning light, I'm sadly certain there was no error in communication.

The only error was one of judgment.

Mine.

Thinking he'd show.

Drawing a deep, frustrated breath, I peer at my watch once more, then raise my face, searching the crowds that wander past the circular aquatic display at Manhattan's epicenter for the performing arts. This fountain is so romantic; that's why we chose it as the place to meet again.

One week later.

Foolishly I hunt for the amber eyes and dark wavy hair, for the lean, tall frame, for that mischievous grin that melts me every time.

I listen for the sound of him amidst the melody of voices, wishing to hear his rise above the others, calling my name, apologizing in that sexy accent of his for being late.

My God, Gabriel's accent was a recipe for making a young

woman weak in the knees. That was what he had done to me. The man melted me when I first met him last month in Barcelona at the tail end of my summer of travels across Europe.

When I close my eyes and float back in time, I hear that delicious voice, just a hint of gravel in his tone, and a whole fleet of butterflies chase each other in my belly at the resurgence of that faraway romantic dream.

I open my eyes, trying to blink away the inconvenient intrusion of memory. I should go. It's clear he's not coming tonight.

But, just in case I mixed up the times, maybe I'll give him one more minute. One more look. One more scan of the crowd.

I let the clock tick past eight.

I still don't see him.

I've been here for more than two hours, sitting on the black marble edge of the fountain. Scouring the corners of Lincoln Center. Peering left, then right down Columbus. Circling, like an animal at a zoo—*pathetic modern-day female waiting for male to stay true to his word.*

Sure, one hundred twenty-plus minutes is not much time in the grand scheme of life, but when the person you're waiting for doesn't show, it's a painful eternity of disillusionment.

I wish we had picked midnight to meet because then I'd have an excuse for him. I'd wonder if midnight meant yesterday or perhaps today. But "six in the evening, on the first of the month, as dusk casts its romantic glow over Manhattan"—his words—is perfectly clear.

He was supposed to be on his way to New York for a job. I'd already landed a plum assignment in this city. Fate appeared to have been looking out for us, and so we'd made plans. One week ago, we'd drunk sangria and danced on the sidewalks of Barcelona, to street musicians playing the kind of music that made you want to get close to someone, and he'd cupped my cheek, saying, "I will count down the days, the hours, the minutes until six in the evening on the first day of September."

Then he'd taken me to his room, wearing that dark and dirty look in his hazel eyes. A look that told me how much he wanted me. Words had fallen from his lips over and over that last night in Spain as he'd undressed me, kissed me all over, and sent me soaring. *My Penelope, give me your body. Let me show you pleasure like you've only imagined.*

Cocky bastard.

But he was right. He'd made all my fantasies real.

He'd made love to me with such passion and sensuality that my traitorous body can still remember the imprint of his hands on my skin, the caress of his delicious lips leaving sizzling marks everywhere.

Standing, I run a hand down my pretty red sundress with the tiny white dots and the scoop neck. He loved me in red. One night we'd walked past a boutique that sold dresses like this. He'd wrapped his arms around me from behind and planted soft, sultry kisses on the back of my neck. "You'd look so lovely in that, my Penelope. And even lovelier when I take it off you. Actually, just wear nothing with me."

I'd shuddered then.

I hurt now as the memory snaps cruelly before my eyes.

I turn away from the fountain, swiping a hand across my cheek. The seed of discouragement planted in the first minutes after he failed to appear has sprouted over the two hours I've waited for him. It's twisted into a thorny weed of disappointment that's lodged deep in my chest.

There are no two ways about it. My three-day love affair under the starry Spanish sky with the man who whispered sweet nothings in my ear while he played my body like a virtuoso pianist isn't getting a second act.

Gabriel has my email.

He knows how to reach me.

He chose not to.

Que sera, sera.

I refuse to cry.

With my chin held high, I walk away.

The rest of the night, the hurt deepens, burrowing into my bones.

The next day, shame wraps itself around that weed in my chest, dominating my emotions. Shame for having believed him. For having bought the damn dress. For having hope.

When I open my closet, I swear the red dress laughs at me. I huff, yank it off the hanger, and stuff it in a grocery bag. I grab the pink one I wore the day I met him, then the soft yellow skirt I had on the next day we were together, which made for such easy access. When I pull down the silky blue tank next, I'm walloped with a reminder of his reaction when he first saw me in it.

His eyes had widened, and he'd groaned appreciatively. "Beautiful."

It was all he'd said, then he'd kissed the hollow of my throat and blazed a sensual trail up my neck, along my jawline to my ear, and whispered, "So beautiful in blue."

I'd melted.

I'd believed all his sweet, swoony words. He'd said so many things that had set my skin on fire, that had made my heart hammer, that had made my panties damp.

Even now, as I clutch the clothes I wore with him, then didn't wear with him, goose bumps rise on my flesh. I squeeze my eyes shut and tell myself to burn the house down.

It's the only way.

I leave my apartment, march ten blocks uptown, and donate the bag of clothes to the nearest Salvation Army.

When I return home, I open my laptop and find the folder with the photos I took of the two of us. I'm tempted, so temped to grab a pint of Ben & Jerry's, run my fingers over the pictures, then download Skype and call his number in Europe to ask why the fuck he didn't show.

But I can't be that girl. I start my first job tomorrow. I need to be a responsible grown-up. I can't be the clingy twenty-one-year-old who isn't able to deal with being ditched.

I'm Penelope Jones, and I can handle anything.

I bring the folder to the trash, then I call up his contact information. His email address. His stupid phone number in Spain. I slide his name to the garbage can, too. My finger hovers over the *empty trash* icon for several interminable seconds that somehow spool into a minute.

But as I remember the way I felt last night, all alone at Lincoln Center, it's wholly necessary to stab the icon.

Let him go.

A clean break.

For the next ten years, I do my best to keep him out of my mind.

Until I see him again.

Chapter One

Present day

Shortcake runs free up the steps. She wags her tail the second her white-gloved paws hit the top of the staircase in our building. My sweet little butterscotch Chihuahua-mix glances back from above me, her pink tongue lolling as she pants.

"Show off," I say to her.

Her white-tipped tail vibrates faster and I take that as my cue to bound up the rest of the stairs, my heart still beating hard from our morning run in Central Park. Last summer, when I brought Shortcake home from Little Friends, the animal rescue I run—she'd insisted upon being mine, slathering me in kisses from the second she'd arrived—I never would have imagined she'd also demand to be my running companion. But she's a fast and furious little widget, all seven pounds of her. We're training for a Four-and-Two-Legs-Race that's part of Picnic in the Park to raise money for a coalition of local animal rescues.

When I reach the fourth floor, Shortcake scurries ahead, rushing to the door of the small one-bedroom we share in the upper 90s. It's all ours, and it's near work, so I can't ask for anything more.

With her leash rolled up in one hand, I unlock the door and enter my home. It's my oasis in Manhattan. The walls are painted lavender and yellow, courtesy of a long weekend when my friend Delaney and I went full Martha Stewart and turned the place into a haven of pastels. I'm not normally a pastel girl, but the soothing shades work for me in here. They make me happy.

I like being happy. Crazy, I know.

I fill Shortcake's water dish, and she guzzles nearly all of it down before sprawling on her belly across the cool kitchen floor, arms stretched in front and legs behind, super-dog style.

"By all means, feel free to spend the day lounging," I say to my favorite girl.

She flops to her side.

"I'm totally not jealous of your lifestyle at all," I say as I strip off my exercise clothes then go to take a quick shower.

When I'm done, I grab my phone. I check my daily appointment list as I blow-dry my dark brown hair. Normally, I'm based at the shelter, working with the animals and my volunteers, or heading to the airports to meet the dogs coming in from other states so we can find them homes. Today, though, I need to dress up and put on my best public face. My assistant, Lacey, has set up meetings for me this week with restaurant owners about catering the upcoming picnic. We're in a bit of a bind—the original restaurant slated to cater it had to cancel at the last minute. In a city stuffed with places to feed your face, you might think finding a restaurant is an easy task. But with a date a mere two weeks away, the options narrow quite quickly. So far, my effort to nab an eatery has been a big bust. I've been calling all over town in the last few days, but have yet to come across a restaurant that's both free that day and the right fit.

My quest continues though, since Lacey tracked down four restaurants with openings the day of the picnic. As I twist my hair into a clip, I click on her email.

First up is Dominic Ravini, who runs an Italian joint best known for its "heavenly" spaghetti, Lacey tells me. Bless her. But I just don't think spaghetti is right for a picnic, unless we switch it up to a *Lady and the Tramp* theme.

I peer over at Shortcake. "I'd share a strand of spaghetti with you anytime," I say as I dust on some blush. She thumps her tail against the floor. I take that as a *yes, bring me home pasta for dinner please. With meatballs, of course.*

Next, Lacey writes that I have an appointment with a burrito shop. I give the email a quizzical stare. Though Lacey assures me it's classy, I'm not convinced burritos are the best choice, either. I need to find a restaurant that can strike the perfect balance of sophistication and informality to entice the guests to donate to the shelters but still fit the picnic-in-the-park theme.

That's why I don't hold high hopes for the Indian restaurant she has lined up. Big fan of chana masala here, but I'm not sure it screams *serve me on a paper plate in the park*.

As I reach into my makeup bag, I scroll to the bottom of the email.

The last restaurant with an opening is called *Gabriel's*.

I startle as I read the name and, unexpectedly, my breath catches. *That name.*

I freeze, one hand on the mascara wand, the other holding my phone. Even now, years after my valiant attempt to erase that man from my history, his name alone does something to me.

I've dated since him. I've had a few serious boyfriends. But there's still just something about that man. Maybe that's the curse of experiencing the best sex of your life at age twenty-one. At the time, I figured that sex with Gabriel was so great because I didn't know better. Now, I've learned that sleeping with him was mind-blowing because...sleeping with him was mind-blowing.

Those three nights in Spain were magical, passionate, and beyond sensual. I've tried to implement Gabriel amnesia, but he still lingers in the corners of my mind. Letting go of the mascara tube, I take a breath and tell myself a name is just a name. It's a mere coincidence that this eatery on my list shares the same name.

Except...my Gabriel was a cook. A struggling line cook in a small bistro in Barcelona that summer, planning to move to Manhattan for a job here.

I drop my forehead into my hand as a fresh wave of foolishness crashes over me. What if he's been here all these years? What if he came to New York and simply didn't want to see me? What if we've been sharing the same island for the last decade? What if he was married when we were together? What if he went home to his wife, his girlfriend, his lover?

I forced myself to stop playing this *what if* game ten years ago when he didn't show for our rendezvous. I booted him from my brain and refused to linger on him, and especially on all the possible reasons why he left me alone.

Now, he's all I can think about. I need to know if this Gabriel is *my* Gabriel.

When I google the restaurant, I let out an audible groan.

I blink.

Blink again.

Try to still my shaking fingers.

He's here. He's in Manhattan. After a decade, I'm going to come face-to-face with the man who stole my heart and my body.

I set down my phone and scoop up my dog. "Can I send Lacey instead?"

She licks my cheek in reply.

"Is that a yes, Shortcake? As in, you think I should play hooky and spend the day with you and make Lacey do my dirty work?"

This time she administers a longer tongue-lashing.

"Most of the time I'm completely content with the fact that you don't talk," I tell her. "But today is not one of those days."

The mere possibility of seeing him again sets off a storm of warring emotions and confusion inside me. I don't know what to do about this meeting, what to say to him, how I should act. The one thing I'm certain of is that I *need* a two-way conversation, so I call my friend Delaney as I pace around my small living room.

"Hey there," she shouts over the background clatter of construction. "If you can't hear me it's because they're jackhammering one frigging block away from my spa, which is completely conducive to a restful day of relaxation. Not."

I laugh. "Let me guess. You're walking to work."

"You got it," she says, her normally pretty voice blaring so loudly I have to hold the phone several inches from my ear.

"Speaking of guessing, want to guess who I just found out is on my work schedule today?"

"Tom Hardy? Scott Eastwood? Chris Pine?"

"Henry Cavill," I say, since he's her favorite celebrity. "But seriously, I'm supposed to have a meeting with…" I stop, since I can still hardly believe what I'm about to say. Then I use the nickname we bestowed on Gabriel many moons ago over a bottle of cabernet. "My *international man of mystery*."

She gasps, and it's loud enough for me to hear her over the

racket. "Are you serious?"

I nod. "One hundred percent."

"Okay, hold on," she says, and then ten seconds later, the background noise is sliced away and it's blissfully quiet. "I stepped into the ATM lobby near work. My first massage is in ten minutes, so give me the details."

I dive in and tell her everything I know. "What do I do? Do I go? Do I send Lacey instead? Do I just...*not show*?"

But as I say the last two words, I know I won't do that. I've been on the receiving end of not showing, and I won't stand him up.

"Simple," she says, with authority. "You go."

My stomach drops. Pressing a hand to the wall for balance, I ask, "Are you sure you didn't mean to say I should spend the day working hard at the shelter so that Lacey can have more responsibility overseeing our charitable events?"

Delaney cracks up. "Yes, I'm completely sure I did not say that. Especially since, correct me if I'm wrong, but this is your job, not hers?"

I heave a sigh as I nod. Backing out isn't my style anyway. This is *my* event and *my* responsibility. It's not something I can push off on an assistant who's still learning the ropes. Besides, with one cancellation already, I need to make sure Picnic in the Park comes together. The buck stops with me.

"Yeah, you're right," I say, resigned. "So, um, what do I do? I have no clue how to waltz into his restaurant like he didn't totally devastate me when I stood waiting at Lincoln Center for a man who never showed."

"It's simple," Delaney says in a cool, confident tone.

"How is it simple?"

"Because you're not the same person. You're not that heartbroken twenty-one-year-old about to start a job she did her best to pretend she was going to love because she thought it would please her parents."

"True," I say, some of her confidence rubbing off on me.

I've changed since then. When I went to Spain after college graduation, I was *mostly* sure that I'd be a research analyst on Wall Street. But a small part of me had dreaded that job before it had even started, and that was why I left after only six months. Funny thing—I wasn't the only one to take off from Smith & Holloway. That was the year of exits from the bank, and it became a running joke. First the receptionist, then the human resources manager, then me. "And I love my job now," I say to Delaney, giving myself a pep talk, "and that's why I have to meet with him. Because who cares about him, anyway? The event is more important than his stupid decision to walk away from me."

"Exactly. And you're not the type of woman any sane man should walk away from. So you need to make him eat his heart out."

"I like how you think," I say, a dose of confidence surging through me.

"Leave your hair down, show off that sexy new tattoo, and wear something that makes you look stunning. You look amazing in blue."

I laugh. "He used to say that, too."

"Boom. Done. Get out that royal blue off-the-shoulder top. The sapphire-colored one. Wear it with jeans. Women usually think they need to show their bare legs to be sexy, but a great pair of skinny jeans and heels is hotter than a skirt. Then walk in with your chin held high, like you don't care that he broke your heart."

A grin spreads across my face. "Perfect. That's the opposite of how I dressed when I knew him." I was all about sundresses and cute little skirts when he met me. Young and innocent.

It's time to dress like the woman I am, not the girl I was.

I say good-bye and open my closet. I want to be so goddamn memorable that his jaw drops from the shock, that he falls to his knees and begs forgiveness for standing me up, that he tells me he hasn't gone a day without thinking of me.

Oh yes, I wish for Gabriel to regret with every fiber of his being that he left me alone on what should have been the most romantic reunion of two summer lovers ever.

I slip into my favorite jeans then adjust the shoulder on the top to show off the lily tattoo on my shoulder blade. As I slide my feet into a pair of black flats, I grab my favorite black heels and drop them into my bag. No need to kill myself in four-inch shoes until I arrive at my final meeting.

On the way to my first appointment, I use my phone to take an online crash course in Gabriel Mathias. Since I don't follow the restaurant scene, I had no idea he'd set up shop here. Turns out he's now something of a rising rock-star chef, who recently won a season of a popular reality TV cooking show, then a few months ago he rode that spot of fame to open his first Manhattan establishment. It's the flagship for a bigger business he now runs in cookware, cookbooks, and more.

Well, la-de-dah. The once-struggling cook who excelled at paella has gone from rags to riches.

I grit my teeth when I see the first photo of him. He's still gorgeous. Actually, I should revise that. He's even more gorgeous.

The fucker.

But I'm not going to let his looks soften me. I'm not going to be swayed by his pretty face. I'm strong, and I'm tough, and I'm smart, too. Which means I need to be prepared.

I find a clip from his show on YouTube as I walk along Eighth Avenue. Popping in my headphones, I hit play and brace myself.

Do not let that sexy accent woo you. Do not stare at those kissable lips.

I do my best to listen objectively, as if he's a test subject in a lab. A host or producer off-camera asks him a question. "You lost tonight's appetizer battle. What do you think that does for your chances to win it all?"

"It makes it tougher for me to win," he says in that warm, sexy voice I adored. "But I'm ready for the challenge. I'll need to work harder on the main course match."

I scoff as I march down the sidewalk. What will these reality geniuses come up with next? Salad showdown? Dessert skirmish?

"How did you feel losing to Angelique when you've been making a name for yourself as a master of appetizers?"

Gabriel takes a breath, his chest rising and falling. Then the corner of his lips curves up. "I was frustrated with myself but not so angry that I'd have, say, thrown a phone."

A laugh comes from off-camera, and I can only imagine the producers huddled together to try to incite him to throw a phone over a fallen flan, or a run-of-the-mill risotto.

The screen flashes, and the video clip cuts to what looks to be the end of the episode with the host holding Gabriel's hand high in the air. I guess he won the match in the end, and his phone was safe from damage.

As I stop at the crosswalk, I return to my original search. My eyes widen when I dig deeper and find stories of his official win on the cooking show, and all the names the media bestowed on him.

The sexiest chef.

The hottest cook.

The heartbreaker in the kitchen.

Nearly every article comes with a photo of him. I click on the first few. Then another set. Then one more group of pics. My chest burns with annoyance. My muscles tighten with anger.

In every single picture of the chef du jour, he has a different woman on his arm.

That's my answer as to why he never showed. Gabriel is a ladies' man. A bad boy. The consummate playboy, out with a new beautiful babe every single night.

As I head in to my meeting with the Italian chef, I hope against hope this man can do something amazing with spaghetti at a picnic so I can call off the rest of my appointments.

He can't.

Then, it turns out the burrito man is now booked for another event.

At the Indian restaurant, the manager tells me it would be his first time catering an event, and he can only cook for fifty. We're expecting more than three hundred. I thank him with a smile, then sigh heavily as I leave and head to the Village to see the man who swept me off my feet once upon a time.

As the train chugs into the station, I change my shoes then tug on my top, showing a bit more shoulder than I usually do. He *loved* to kiss me there. He loved tattoos, too. I didn't have any then. I have three now, including the lily. Let him look. Let him stare.

I slick on lip gloss as I leave the subway, check my reflection in the shop window on the corner, and make my way to Gabriel's on Christopher Street. My heart beats double time.

When I reach the brick-front eatery on the corner of two cobbled streets, I'm more impressed than I want to be. His restaurant is so cool and hip and sexy, with a dash of old-fashioned charm in the hanging wooden sign.

I narrow my eyes and nearly breathe a plume of fire onto the entryway. He probably charms the female patrons with his witty words, his panty-melting grin, and his fucking amazing food.

Then takes them to his bed and runs his tongue…

Stop. Just stop.

I clench my fists then take a breath, letting it spread through my body. I remind myself I'm here for business. I'm here for the dogs. This is my chance to raise a lot of money for a cause that matters dearly to me.

When the hostess greets me and I tell her I have a meeting with Gabriel, a part of me hopes that he's grown a paunch, acquired a receding hairline, or perhaps lost a tooth in a barroom brawl.

But as he strides toward where I wait by the door, the saying *take my breath away* means something entirely new.

Oxygen flees my body.

The twenty-four-year-old guy who dazzled me when I gave him my virginity a decade ago has nothing on this man in front of me.

He's as beautiful as heartbreak. With cheekbones carved by the masters, eyes the color of topaz, and hair that's now shoulder-length, he's somehow impossibly sexier. My fingers itch to touch those dark strands. My skin sizzles as images of him moving over me flicker fast before my eyes.

I try to focus on the here and now, but the here and now makes my heart hammer with desire. Everything about him exudes confidence, charm, and sex appeal, even his casual clothes. He wears black jeans, lace-up boots, and a well-worn V-neck T-shirt that reveals his lean, toned, inked arms. He had several when I knew him—now his arms are nearly covered in artwork, and they're stunning. His ink is so incredibly seductive.

He holds out a hand and flashes me that grin that makes me want to grab the neck of his shirt, yank him close, and say *kiss me now like you did all those nights before.*

Instead, he takes my palm in his then presses his lips to the top of my hand, making my head spin. Then he speaks, his accent like an opiate. He's French and Brazilian, and I don't know which side dominates his voice. I don't care, either, because the mixture of the two is delicious. "I've been looking forward to seeing you, Penny."

Oh God. Oh shit. He's excited to see me.

My stupid heart dances.

I swallow, trying to tap in to the section of my brain that's capable of language. I part my lips, but my mouth imitates the Sahara.

I dig down deep, somehow finding the power of speech, and manage a parched, "Hello."

So much for playing it cool.

"Shall we sit down?" he asks, his delicious voice as sensual as it was that summer.

Yes, and tell me you're sorry. Tell me you were trapped in a cave, that spies stole your phone, that you were offered the job of the century in Nepal and you couldn't bear to see me again because then you'd never have taken the gig. You had no choice, clearly. Seeing me would have made it impossible to resist me.

Because that would be him eating his goddamn heart out.

Instead, I'm greeted with another enchanting smile as he says, "It's so good to meet you. I want to hear all about your charity and to see if we can work together for your event. My business manager believes this could be a great partnership for us both." He gestures to a quiet booth in the far corner. The lunchtime rush hasn't begun. I sit, then he slides across from me.

As I begin to share information with him about Little Friends, a fresh, cold wave of understanding washes over me.

He doesn't recognize me, and I honestly don't look that different than I did ten years ago.

Which means…he doesn't remember me.

Chapter Two

Gabriel

As I head to the kitchen to grab a plate I've already prepared for her, something in the back of my mind nags at me, like someone is poking me, trying to tell me something. Maybe rustle up a memory best forgotten. It's on the tip of my tongue. The edge of my fingers.

Pressing my hands to the steel counter, I close my eyes and let my mind slip back in time. A beautiful face flashes past me, and I wish I had photos of her. She took many, and was supposed to send them to me, but I never heard from her again.

I open my eyes and shake my head. There's no way that woman at the booth is *her*. Surely, she would have said something. She doesn't use the same name. She uses a variation of it that the woman I'd known swore she'd never use. Penny. "Penny doesn't fit a Wall Street analyst. But Penelope does," she'd said.

But that was ten years ago. Maybe she changed her mind. She might very well go by Penny now.

Except Penny—the woman at the table—isn't a Wall Street analyst.

I snag the white-and-blue dish and return to the booth. I present it to Penny—the woman who manages an animal shelter and does *not* run reports on stocks—with a flourish. "Try it. It's a specialty sandwich. I made it just for you."

Her eyelids flutter. "For me?"

I flash her a smile. "Of course I made it for you. I want you to experience what I can do," I say, and she blushes. The prettiest shade of light red splashes across her cheeks, so I quickly add, "What I can do for your event, of course."

She drops her gaze to the plate, regarding the mini sandwich. "It looks amazing."

"It tastes even better," I say, leaning back in the booth. I'm not short on confidence in the cooking department. Even so, I want her to love it. "It's a variation on a Bauru, a traditional Brazilian sandwich. Roast beef, French bread, pickled cucumbers, but with a few new ingredients to give it a special flair."

She picks it up and takes a small bite. Her eyes sparkle as she chews. And yes, she looks sexy eating my food. I can't think of much that's more sensual than a beautiful woman enjoying what I've concocted for her. And Penny is a most beautiful woman. Long, lush hair. Warm, inviting eyes. A red mouth ripe for kissing.

As I watch her, I do more than look—I *study* her face. That gnawing reminder reappears in my brain, a little voice telling me I know her.

That faraway face glimmers once more in my mind. Penny's hair falls in soft waves, curling at the ends. But hers is darker than the hair from the image in my mind, and so much longer. Hair changes, I know. But still, I try desperately to connect the two women—to make sense of the images in my mind. The woman I'm picturing—the woman I had to banish from my thoughts years ago—was so young, so fresh-faced, with lighter hair that hit her jawline and an innocent smile that knocked me to my knees. This woman is more…sophisticated. It's an alluring look, though, one that captivated me from the second she walked into my restaurant.

I didn't get her last name when my business manager set up this appointment. Just Penny. But she reminds me so much of the woman I met in Spain and spent the best three nights of my life with.

If she's one and the same, why didn't she say something when she arrived? Maybe because Penny's not Penelope. She's not in the same line of work. Banking and charitable work aren't exactly the same field.

She nods several times as she finishes, then points to the rest of the sandwich. "This is absolutely incredible. I could eat it every day and never tire of it."

I beam, soaking in her praise like sunshine as I try to figure out the mystery of her. "Thank you. I'm glad you like it."

"No, I don't just like it," she says, shaking her head adamantly. "I *love* it. It's a..." She pauses as if she's searching for the words. "A heavenly sandwich."

And my grin extends to the next state. "I couldn't be more pleased that you feel this way." But my mind returns to Barcelona as I remember the woman there heaping praise like this upon a dessert we shared. "It's divine," she'd said that day. I shove aside the fleeting memory. "It would be perfect for your picnic event, wouldn't it? We need an amazing dessert, though."

She doesn't answer right away. She almost seems reluctant when she utters a yes, then follows it with, "It would be. And we do." Something in her tone sounds wistful, and it tugs at my memory once more.

I simply must know if I'm seeing double.

"Have you ever been to Miami?" I blurt out. Maybe I met her there at my other restaurant, and my mind is fooling me that she's the woman I couldn't find at that fated time ten years ago.

She frowns in confusion. "Yes, but many years ago."

I lean closer to the table, soften my voice. "Forgive me, but you look so familiar..."

Her eyes widen, and something vulnerable seems to flash in them. She brings a hand to her hair. "I do?"

I nod vigorously. "Yes. So much. It's eerie."

She swallows. "We all remind each other of others, don't we?"

"Perhaps we do," I say. I'm not sure what to make of her answer so I return to the matter at hand, telling her more of what I would make for her charity fundraiser. My business manager, Eduardo, alerted me to this opportunity the other day when it landed on his desk. With my new restaurant opening a few months ago, I've been looking to make a splash in Manhattan. Reviews have been amazing and business has been robust, but I know that fortunes can turn on a dime. Hell, do I ever fucking know that. "And I would make the most fantastic desserts for you, too," I say with a wink, because that reminds me of the afternoon I met the girl in Barcelona—we'd both been eating dessert at a street-side café, where we'd started flirting. "Desserts are my specialty."

"What would you make?" she asks, then she murmurs *oh God*

when I tell her what I'd create for the sweetest course. The soft sound she makes stirs something in my chest, then sends a rush of heat below the belt. That sense of déjà vu sharpens, and a reel of images snaps before my eyes, like puzzle pieces fighting to connect.

I scrub a hand over my jaw, arching an eyebrow. It's driving me crazy. "Are you sure we've never met?"

Her eyes seem to twinkle. She shifts closer, her top sloping farther off her shoulder. My eyes follow that move, catching on to the ink there. Jesus Christ. It's so fucking hot I want to run my tongue over it, like I do the rest of her.

"I think the question is—are *you* sure we've never met?" Her tone is playful and it reels me in, like she did that first afternoon. The mere possibility that she's one and the same thrills me.

I drag a finger along my lower lip as I remember what it was like to kiss that girl. How she seemed to melt when I touched her. "You look exactly like someone…" I angle my shoulders closer, zeroing in only on her, as the noise and the clatter of the kitchen behind me seems to fade away. "Someone I knew once, years ago."

Her lips twitch in the hint of a smile. "And who is this girl you once knew?"

"She was—"

"Hello there, handsome."

Before I can finish and tell her "someone I desperately wanted to see again," the moment collapses when Greta speaks. I turn to the curvy blonde I see nearly every day. A box of produce is balanced on her hip. "Hello there, Greta," I say. "Have you brought me all sorts of goodies today?"

Greta pats the box. "Only the best for you. I have strawberries and cantaloupes and some peaches too," she says in a purr, making everything sound like innuendo. She's just like that. She's a flirt, but it's never been more than this with her—this playful banter.

"Mmm, peaches," I say, then cock my head to Penny. "Do you like peaches?"

For a moment, I picture sliding a slice of a peach between those lips and watching her lick it, bite it, savor it.

In a cool tone, she answers, "Who doesn't like peaches?"

"It's a sin not to like peaches. May I have one now, please?" I say to Greta, and she hands me one, leaning close enough to show a peek of her cleavage.

"A peach for you, Gabriel," Greta says, letting my name roll off her tongue. She mouths, "See you later, handsome," just like she always does.

"*Merci*," I tell her, then she saunters into the kitchen with the daily delivery. I turn my focus back to Penny, whose expression is hard to read. I gesture in Greta's direction. "Greta handles my produce."

Her lips curve up, but she's not exactly smiling. "I bet she does."

I furrow my brow because the comment sounded almost...*salty.* "Excuse me?"

Penny seems to transform her expression in an instant, smiling as she says sweetly, "I bet she does a great job."

I take the knife on the table and slice open the peach, cutting it into chunks. "She does. But back to what I was saying—you look so familiar. Every single thing about you," I say, trying once more. "Penny..." My voice trails off as I grasp at her name, waiting for her to supply *Jones.*

"Penny Smith." She's all business as she answers, and there goes my hope. "And yes, I understand how that can be. But I assure you, Gabriel, we've never met."

"*C'est la vie,* then," I say with a shrug. "But we know each other now, and I look forward to working with you, Penny Smith."

"I'm delighted that you're free for the event. I think we can raise so much money to help the local animals by working together, don't you?"

"I absolutely do." I offer her a slice of the fruit. "Try it. I promise you won't regret it."

"I'm sure I won't regret it, either, since I don't believe in regret when it comes to peaches," she says, her tone dry.

I tilt my head, trying to make sense of her comment as she grabs the slice from my fingers then pops it in her mouth. A small, sexy murmur slips from her lips as she bites the fruit. I can't stop watching her eat. I can't stop looking at her. I can't stop staring.

When she finishes, she says, "Yes, the peaches seem to have been handled well." She scoots out of the booth and extends a hand for me to shake. "I'm so glad you're on board. I'll have my assistant, Lacey, follow up."

Quickly, I push to my feet and take her hand. "Wait. Are you going?"

She nods crisply. "Yes. I need to leave. You're sure you're free the date of the event in the park?"

I nod. "I'm sure."

"You don't have anything else planned?"

I shake my head. "I don't."

"The other restaurant we had booked for this cancelled a few days ago. The chef at least called me and told me, though."

"That was good of him to give you notice. But I assure you, I will be there. That is, if you want to work together."

"Absolutely. I need you," she says. Then, as if she's correcting herself, she adds, "We need you."

"I'm glad to be able to do this. But we should talk again. About the menu. Go over it. Review it," I say. My words come out more nervously than I expect, but the prospect of her walking away feels strangely unsettling.

"We could chat on the phone," she offers.

That won't do. "Let's talk over dinner. Tonight."

"Don't you need to cook?"

I gesture to our surroundings—the tables and chairs, the kitchen behind me, the hostess stand. "I don't do all the cooking anymore, since I'm running the business, too. But I will still work all day and prep the sauces and plan the specials. I have an amazing sous chef who'll cook tonight."

She offers a small smile. "I can't tonight. I'm busy."

"Tomorrow?" I won't back down. I need to see her again.

"I have plans then."

"The next night?"

She takes a breath, then gives a half nod and says, a touch reluctantly, "Sure."

"Where do you live?"

She points north. "Upper West Side."

"What is your favorite food?"

"Spanish," she says, her eyes locked on mine and full of meaning. The look in her amber eyes is a challenge. But I like challenges, and I'm up to this one.

"Excellent. I know just the place to take you," I say, and give her the name of the restaurant I have in mind. "Eight p.m. Friday. Can you be there?"

Something sad passes in her eyes, then she answers. "I'll be there."

I hold up a finger to tell her to wait and rush to the hostess stand to grab a piece of paper and a pen. I write on it and hand the paper to Penny, the dead ringer for Penelope, but that's all. "My number. If you're running late."

"I won't be late."

"If you were, I'd wait for you."

She purses her lips, as if she's holding back. "I'll see you Friday."

"Do you want to give me your number?"

"I'll text it to you," she says and she leaves, but she doesn't send me her number.

I spend the rest of the day bouncing between the kitchen here and the offices of my company a few blocks away, and I can't get Penny out of my mind. I can't stop thinking about her lips, her eyes, her voice, and the way they're playing with my head, like a dream.

She feels like one—wispy, beautiful, just out of reach. The kind you want to be real, but when you wake up, you're merely clutching to the hem of a cloud as it floats away.

Chapter Three

Penny

"No clue," I say, slicing a hand through the air. "He had no clue."

Delaney gives me a side-eye stare, complete with a fully arched eyebrow. "Sounded like he actually had a pretty good clue and you denied it," she says as Shortcake trots over to a chocolate-brown mastiff in the dog park at West 87th and the Hudson River. We lean against the fence inside the park, and I wave to Mitch, the mastiff's owner, a wiry guy with glasses and dirty blond hair. The guy waves back.

My tiny dog stands tall on her hind legs and bats the big dog's face as best she can. To help her out, the mastiff bends his top half down to the ground, his hindquarters in the air. It's the perfect giant-meets-the-pipsqueak playing position.

I point at my girl. "I want to be just like her."

"Boxing the big boys?"

"Yup."

Delaney nods, her high, blond ponytail swishing back and forth. "Don't we all? She's the underdog who's now—what do we call her? The overdog?"

I laugh as Shortcake play-fights the dog who's easily fifteen times her weight. "She'd approve of that description."

Delaney turns and looks me in the eye. "Seriously, though, Pen. Why didn't you admit it was you?"

I shrug, trying to make light of what happened yesterday at Gabriel's restaurant. "Just wasn't feeling it."

She elbows me. "C'mon. That's lame. You're not a *just wasn't feeling it* person."

Like that, my best friend busts me.

The truth is, it's hard to make light of seeing Gabriel again because every second with him felt like we were on the cusp of something, like a storm cloud swollen with rain before it bursts. I didn't admit who I was because I didn't want to get caught in the downpour. "I was going to," I explain. "I swear. He seemed so legit when he kept asking if we knew each other, and it made me *want* to tell him. I was just waiting for *him* to fully make the connection. I didn't want to do all the work."

"I get that. Truly, I do." She sets her hand on my arm. Delaney is a tactile person. She's always touching. Makes sense, since she does massage for a living. "And I'm all for making the man suffer. But from what you told me, it sounds like he was trying hard to connect the dots."

I point to my face. "You've known me forever. Do I look *that* different?"

She tilts her head to the side and taps her chin. "Hmm. Penelope Jones, the twenty-one-year-old Wall Street research analyst with the short news-anchor haircut? Or Penny Jones, lover of music and dogs, who abandoned the financial business after half a year to pursue her dream of working with animals and at thirty-one now has crazy long hair and tattoos along her shoulder?" She pauses to add, "Or Penny Smith now, evidently."

I hold up my hands in surrender. "I gave him the wrong name at that point because I didn't want to open myself up to hearing whatever bullshit excuse he was going to give me," I say, trying to stay tough. The full truth is I would have been hurt all over again in a new, fresh way if he'd connected the dots and then said something nonchalant like, "Oh, sorry. I couldn't make it to Lincoln Center that night. I was busy making a roast."

Delaney levels her gaze at me. "What happens when you're working together on the event and he refuses to deny anymore that it's you?"

Her point is valid. But I'm not sure I'm ready to face that possibility. "I was going to say something. I was planning on telling him who I was. But then Greta the fruit lady, with her very own cantaloupes for breasts, appeared, and she was so flirty with him," I say, seething as I picture the busty woman. "She called him handsome then said 'see you later,' and well, obviously there's something going on with them."

Delaney scoffs. "That doesn't sound obvious at all. Maybe she's just flirty and he's just friendly with people he works with."

I huff, hardly wanting to admit she may be right. "Be that as it may, what would have been the point? He believed he didn't know me. I didn't need to open the old wound. I've done a pretty good job of putting what happened with him behind me. I've moved on. Lord knows I needed to."

Her narrow-eyed look tells me she doesn't believe me. "I don't know if you've completely moved on. If you'd moved on, I think you'd have told him." Her tone softens. "Just playing devil's advocate."

"It didn't seem worth the time."

"Then why did you say yes to dinner with him?"

I look away from her and watch the dogs play. The mastiff rolls onto his back, his front legs in the air. Shortcake paws his snout from that position. Mitch laughs loudly then returns to his phone.

"She's so cute," I say as I stare at my dog.

Delaney laughs loudly. "Oh my God, you still want him."

I snap my gaze back at her. "Mitch?" I ask under my breath, casting my eyes toward the blond, bespectacled man. "We went on two dates and agreed we were better off as dog park friends."

Mitch had asked me out a few months ago, and he's lovely and funny and sweet, but we have very little in common besides dogs.

Delaney shakes her head. "No. I mean Gabriel. *Obviously.*"

"Please."

"Why else would you want to go to dinner with him?"

"For work," I say, insistently. Perhaps too insistently.

She nudges her shoulder into mine. "He's still gorgeous, isn't he?"

"No," I say, denying the truth.

She shakes her head, her lips quirking up. "You so love bad boys."

"*You* love bad boys," I toss back.

She holds up her hands. "Never denied it."

"Besides," I huff, "I said yes because we have to plan the event."

She nods, with skeptical eyes that say she doesn't believe me. "You said yes to dinner because you want him to remember you. You want him to say he's sorry. You want him to grovel."

I heave a sigh. "Stop being a mind reader."

She flashes me a smile. "One of my many talents. But I have a serious question for you. Did you not admit it was you because of him...or because of Gavin?"

My nose crinkles at the mention of my ex. "Let's not speak of the cad."

"The cad you almost married. Thank God you dodged that bullet."

I shoot her a withering stare. "I did *not* almost marry him."

Delaney taps her forehead. "But you thought about it." She shudders in horror. "I'm glad he showed his true colors. He deserves to be strung up by his—"

I cover her mouth with my hand. "Don't say it. I don't want to think of his parts in any context. It'll just remind me what he did with them and where he put them."

Gavin, a regular donor to Little Friends, was my last serious boyfriend. I was sure he was going to propose. I wasn't entirely sure what I was going to say. I had loved him, but I wasn't convinced that he was the one. And near the end, I'd had the sense that I wasn't the only one at all for him. A pilot, he was one of those roguishly handsome captains who made women swoon. In New York. In Los Angeles. In Chicago. In Dallas. He had a lady in every port. When I learned about his out-of-the-cockpit escapades, he tried to grovel his way back into my heart but I kicked him out. I didn't want to hear his excuses, so I sent his things to his work address and told him to "buckle up as it might be a bumpy landing." I was tough and take-no-prisoners on the outside, but then I licked my wounds with Ben & Jerry's, badass breakup tunes, long runs in the park, and lots of Purple Snow Globe cocktails with Delaney.

I sigh. "I would just like to find a man who's like a dog. Someone who's loyal."

Out of the corner of my eye, I spot the mastiff now cavorting with a German shepherd, chasing the brown and tan dog around the edge of the park. Meanwhile, Shortcake tugs on the ear of a basset hound. Delaney and I crack up in unison. "Or maybe not," she says.

"But in all seriousness, I guess I just thought it would be easier by now," I say, turning all philosophical for a moment. "Love, you know?" She nods, and I continue, "Back when I was twenty-one and I fell for Gabriel in Spain, it seemed like it had the potential to become something real. I was young and foolish, and it lasted only three days, so maybe that was my fault for wanting more. But it really hurt when he didn't show up." I raise my chin. "I'm a big girl. I moved on. I've had some good experiences and some bad experiences. I'm not complaining, but what I'd really like is to have just one amazing experience with someone that lasts a lifetime. Is that possible anymore in this day and age?"

Delaney shakes her head ruefully. "Don't ask me. The things I hear from my clients all day long…"

In her job, Delaney is privy to all sorts of tales. She's told me the wild stories her clients share as they relax under her magic touch, their loose tongues revealing sordid stories of affairs, trysts, ménages, online crushes, and late-night secret rendezvous. "Sometimes I think we're better off single."

Maybe we are. Maybe we're better off by ourselves, with our dogs and our friends, than with a guy who maintains a little black book as he flies, or with a playboy who reappears in our lives.

As I ponder dating and mating and truths and lies, a beautiful russet-coated Irish Setter mix rushes into the park, bounding through the beasts. Her name is Ruby, and all the canine heads turn and immediately follow her.

Right behind Ruby is her owner, who is perfectly paired with her pet. Nicole has a mane of silky red hair that matches her dog's gorgeous coat. She's tall, beautiful, and brimming with confidence. When she spots us, she waves and calls out a hello. She heads over and gives me a big hug, then says hi to Delaney, too. The mastiff follows her and wags his tail as he rubs his haunches against her thigh.

"He has a crush on you," Delaney says, gesturing to the big dog.

Nicole laughs and scratches the dog's chin. "He's just a lover. He loves all the ladies, doesn't he?"

"Sounds like someone else I know," I mutter.

Nicole arches an eyebrow. "Gavin? Is he trying to win you back again? Didn't he send you an email asking for another chance?"

I shake my head. "That was a month ago. I suspect he had a layover in New York and wanted a lay more than a do-over. I ignored him."

Nicole's mouth forms an *O*. "Ooh, he'll need some aloe vera for that burn."

Delaney jumps in. "But it's not him this time. She's beyond Gavin. Penny saw someone she used to have a thing for many years ago."

Nicole parks her hands on her hips and gives me a sharp stare. "Now, what did I tell you about that, young lady?"

Nicole often dispenses relationship advice. The first adage she ever shared was about her long-lost engagement ring.

I scratch my head and try to remember which love lesson might apply to my situation. "Is this like your what-it-means-when-you-lose-a-ring scenario?"

She raises a hand and shakes her index finger. "No. But that advice is not only golden—it's platinum. Like the ring that went bye-bye."

Delaney pantomimes a rim shot.

The redhead takes a quick bow. "Thank you, ladies. Be sure to tip the waiters on the way out." Then she squares her shoulders. "But seriously, Penny. It's this: life is too short to waste on exes. They're usually exes for a reason."

Later that evening, as Shortcake curls up on my lap on the couch while I assemble a new playlist of indie tunes on my phone, I return to Nicole's advice, wondering the true reason why Gabriel is an ex.

I've never known the reason. Maybe I don't want to know.

But if I'm being honest with myself, and I like to think I am, I suppose I *do* want to know.

That's why I reach into my purse, unfold the sheet of paper with his number, and enter the digits into my phone. I take a breath and do something I haven't done in a decade.

I send him a message.

Chapter Four

Gabriel

The knife gleams in Tina's hand.

"Like this?" My neighbor curls her fingers above the red onion in her left hand, holding the sharp blade in her right.

"Perfect," I say with a wide smile, as the soaring chorus of a rock song crashes through the state-of-the-art sound system in her apartment.

Tina lowers the shiny metal and cuts a fine, thin slice. I hold my arms out wide as the singer croons about love lost. "See? You will be my sous in no time."

Tina arches a silver brow. "Just like you will become my student."

I laugh and drop a kiss to her wrinkled forehead. My new neighbor is a world-renowned cellist. After three decades traveling the world and playing classical music so beautifully that audiences wept, Tina retired recently, finishing her career with the New York Philharmonic. Because of her nomadic life, she never learned to cook for herself. That wasn't an issue when she was married. But she's now a widow, since her husband died last year. When I moved to Manhattan and into the building earlier this summer, Tina and I hit it off, and soon she was passing along tips about which washing machine in the basement was always on the fritz and which delivery service was the most reliable, while I wound up helping around her home. I've fixed her sink disposal, changed some lightbulbs, and hung a picture frame.

When she confessed she'd never once made a meal on the stove, I set about rectifying that with cooking lessons. One of the first things I taught her was how to hold a knife properly, and she's got it down pat now. As she finishes chopping the vegetables for her stir-fry, I glance at the wall clock.

"I need to go soon, Tina. But this weekend, don't forget, I will take you to the farmer's market in Union Square and we'll pick out the best vegetables for a pasta primavera."

"Is that an official date, then, with the sexiest chef in Manhattan?" She winks, and I shake my head, bemused. She will never let me live down my stint on that reality show. It entertains her to no end. "And then I'll teach you how to play Bach's *Cello Suite Number One*."

I laugh. "Somehow, I think you'll learn to cook much faster than I'll ever learn to hit one correct note on a cello. You are the true master. But maybe you can tell me who we're listening to," I say, pointing in the direction of her speakers. "I like this music."

"Ah," she says with a nod. She sets down the knife on the cutting board. "You're learning fast that I'm good for more than Brahms and Tchaikovsky. This is Pizza for Breakfast."

I crack up. "Seriously? That's really a band name?"

Indignant, she says, "And a damn good one. Don't make fun of Pizza for Breakfast. They're local, and they're playing at the Den this weekend."

I smack my palm on my forehead. "What has the world come to when I actually like a band called Pizza for Breakfast?"

She parks her hands on her hips. "Now, don't tell me you dislike pizza for breakfast as a food. That was my staple for years."

"I love pizza any time of the day, Tina, and I like this band. I'll download the music later."

"Pay for it, young man."

"Do I look like a pirate?"

"Not tonight, in your fancy shirt. By the way, who's the date with?"

I wrench back, surprised at her comment. "I didn't mention a date."

She smirks, a knowing glint in her warm brown eyes. "You didn't have to. I can tell from your clothes," she says, eyeing my attire.

My eyes drift down to my shirt, a dark blue button-down. "But see, I look devilishly handsome every day. Tonight is no different."

"You dressed up more tonight. You're usually in those too-tight jeans and an oh-so-trendy T-shirt—"

"I've never had any complaints about my jeans. Or my shirts, for that matter."

"As I was saying, judging from this dress shirt, either you're wooing investors, which I know you're not, or you're seeing a woman you like more than usual," she says in that sharp, motherly tone she sometimes takes with me.

I shrug an admission.

"Has the ladies' man of the kitchen met someone special?" she asks saucily, firing off one of the many names tacked on me over the years. There's no point denying it. The names are true, though it's a bit of a chicken-and-egg situation. When I first rose up in the ranks, somehow the food and dining press was as interested in my dating life as my cuisine. On the reality show, which I desperately needed to land a spot on, the producers made it clear that they liked that many of the women wanted my food and *also* wanted to go home with me. I'm not complaining about the opportunities that have come my way, especially since they've often intersected with the skyrocketing of my career.

In the last few years, I've been a lucky man, but I've known the other side of luck, too, and I don't mean in love. I mean in life. As I was growing up, my family had very little. We scraped by for everything. My Brazilian father, an artist, fell in love with my French mother, a teacher, when he studied in France. We didn't have much, but my parents rarely complained. Nor did I, even as I worked my ass off, desperately seeking the TV job and the chance it might afford me to leapfrog my career.

It worked, and now I run three restaurants, as well as a company that's expanding into cookware, cookbooks, and more. That's why I moved to New York from Miami a few months ago, since New York was better suited for the expansion.

And so, the nicknames have followed me—playboy chef, sexiest chef, and more.

"I'm hardly a ladies' man," I say to Tina.

"You can't fool me, Gabriel," she says, as she reaches for a bell pepper from a basket on her counter. "But answer the question, or I'll cook my peppers too long and claim that's what you taught me."

I feign a look of horror. "Not that. Never." The music shifts to a softer tune, and I pause to listen as a new voice sounds. "This band is good, too." Then I add, "Anyway, it's not a date."

"Liar."

I sigh. "Fine. You win. She's someone I'm working with on a charity event."

"But you want to impress her for more than the event?" Tina says, like she can see right through me.

Denial is impossible with her. She's one of those women who just *knows* stuff. "Perhaps I do."

"What makes her special?"

My mind roams back to Penny, and a smile tugs at my lips as I recall the twenty minutes we spent together at a booth in my restaurant the other day. "Besides being beautiful, I presume?"

Tina laughs sagely. "Beauty fades. Tell me about *her*."

"I barely know her, but she's sharp and passionate," I say, remembering her "heavenly sandwich" compliment and the way she'd teased me, too, asking me if I was sure I knew her. I'd been certain at first, then perhaps not so much at all. "And more than that, she reminds me of someone."

Tina shakes the pepper at me. "Don't date her because she reminds you of someone else. Date her for her."

"It's not even a date."

Tina scoffs. "Spoken like the sexiest chef in New York. Now go, or you'll be late, and she won't like that." She grabs my arm and she tips her head toward the speakers. "Retractable Eyes. The band."

"Where do they come up with these names?"

"Admit it. You love them."

"They might have a way with notes and melodies," I say, since Tina is nothing if not a musical goddess. I've found many crazy new bands to listen to because of her, and I love giving her a hard time about the wild names bands use today.

I say good-bye, and as I head uptown, I hold tight to Tina's words, as if I'm clutching them in my fist.

Date her for her.

Penny might remind me, in a double-vision kind of way, of my Penelope from years ago, but I'm seeing her tonight for *her*, not for the sweetest memory. Though she sent me a text yesterday evening that reminded me so much of the girl I knew for three magical nights.

I should warn you in advance—I love dessert. This restaurant better bring it in that department.

When I walk into Sabrina's Restaurant, I'm early, and that gives me the chance to grab a spot at the bar and watch for Penny to enter. When the gorgeous brunette with the flower tattoos walks through the door a few minutes later, my throat goes dry.

My blood heats, because she's prettier than I'd thought she was the other day, and I want to catalogue every detail. I rake my gaze over her, from the black heels, to the snug jeans that make her legs look long and sexy, to the bare arms exposed by the strappy silvery tank she wears. Her wrists are covered in slim, metallic bangles, and her lush brown hair is pinned up on one side in a small butterfly clip, showing the delicate ink curving over her shoulder.

I don't need to discuss menus or events with her.

I asked her out tonight because I haven't been this drawn to someone I just met in ten years.

I walk over to her, clasp one hand on her shoulder, and dust a kiss on one cheek, then the other. A soft gust of breath escapes her lips, and she shudders.

I do, too.

Chapter Five

Penny

"Wine?"

Gabriel offers me the wine list, and I take it. There's a part of me that's dying to say, "Yes, let's order a bottle like that last night. Remember how we didn't even finish our glasses because we were dying to be alone? We got the check early and went to your room, and you brought me pleasure the likes of which I haven't come close to having since. But hey, I didn't call you The Yardstick for nothing."

Instead, I swallow my nerves and say, "Any question that starts and ends with *wine* should be answered with *yes*."

He smiles, a ridiculously sexy smile that makes me want both to pump my fist for having nailed a witticism and to lean across the table and kiss that fucking gorgeous grin off his face.

Oh, wait. Let's add a third option. I'd like to take a full dose of I-don't-give-a-fuck attitude so I can walk out in the middle of dinner and leave him here, flustered and confused, at the ridiculously romantic Spanish restaurant with its exposed brick walls and candles on the table. Except, I know I won't do that, and it's not simply because he looks like the cover model for *Bon Appétit*'s "Chefs I Want to Bang" issue.

He's so beautiful, it's criminal. It simply has to be against the law to look the way he does. He has the type of face for billboards, the kind so handsome it should cause traffic pileups from voyeurs staring at his jaw, his lips, his see-inside-my-soul amber eyes. Then he has all that thick, dark hair—he was handsome with short hair, but he's a god with these longer locks, the kind that my hands beg to touch.

To top it all off, he's dressed deliciously tonight—sophisticated, but edgy, too. The cuffs on Gabriel's shirt are rolled up to his elbows, revealing his inked forearms, covered in swirls, lines, and stunning illustrations. Some are new, like the twin tribal bands below his elbow, but the vintage map of the world on his left forearm is so familiar that my chest aches from the memory.

One afternoon, I traced my fingertip over the outline of Europe as we lay on a blanket in Park Güell at the top of Barcelona, surrounded by panoramic views of the city and Gaudi's architectural masterpieces. The grass was cool and soft beneath us, and the air rich with the scent of earth, fragrant summer flowers, and desire.

"I know this continent like the back of my hand," I said, since I'd studied European History in college.

"Show me all the lands." He held out his arm as he challenged me.

My fingers traveled over England, Germany, France, Austria, and Holland, naming each. There were no borders on him. I drew in the countries because I knew them well. I filled in the boundaries of Portugal as it met Spain, where he'd lived for the past few months. When he asked my favorite country, I showed him that, too, by traveling along the outline of a boot. His breath hitched as I traced Italy, and then he said, his voice husky with need, "Kiss me, my Penelope."

I can hear those words echo across time.

"Do you have a favorite?" he asks, the wine list spread out in front of him at this tiny table.

"Italy," I murmur, before I realize the word has fallen from my mouth. I blink, startled back to the present, and I raise my face and meet his eyes.

He tilts his head, his expression quizzical.

I try to cover up my slip-of-the-tongue. "Italian wine, I mean. But I guess they don't have it here, being a Spanish restaurant. I'll say my favorite is sangria," I say, then my lips curve into a grin. "Except you can't order that with a chef."

His eyes twinkle. "Do you think I'm a wine snob? That I don't like sangria?"

My lips part to answer, but I stop. The truth is I don't know. I assumed he would be against it, since sangria is such a punch bowl wine. I go for honesty. "I don't know. I suppose I thought you'd want something fancy."

"Just because I cook doesn't mean I dislike pizza, or sandwiches, or a simple sangria. Do *you* like sangria is the more important question?"

Right now, I just need something, anything, to quench my thirst. "I love it. And I'd love a Tempranillo, too," I say, naming a more sophisticated wine, lest he think I'm uneducated about the world he lives in—the finer things in life.

But, oh shit. I just requested two drinks. God, I sound like a lush. Why don't I ask him to thrust a glass in each of my hands, so I can double-fist and guzzle till I pass out?

Thankfully, the waiter arrives, and Gabriel orders a glass of each. When the man leaves, my dinner companion shoots me a knowing grin. "We can share, since I like both."

Share.

Like we did the dessert when we met at the café.

Tingles spread across my bare shoulders, evoked both from the past and from the present. From the memory of the day we met and split a Tarta de Santiago almond cake with a caramel layer on the bottom, and the here and now as we share wine. When the waiter brings our two red beverages, Gabriel slides the sangria to me first. "I have a feeling it's what you really wanted."

You're what I really want.

"Maybe I secretly craved the Tempranillo," I tease.

He gestures to both. "Ladies first, then. Have your pick."

I take a drink of the Tempranillo. It's both sweet and sharp. "It tastes like cherry and black pepper," I say, adopting a faux snooty tone.

He laughs. "We have a wine connoisseur on our hands, I see."

Wrapping my arms around the glass, I pretend I'm hoarding the Tempranillo. "This is delicious, and I shall keep it all to myself."

He laughs, leaning his head back and running a hand through his hair. My eyes follow his fingers and their destination. This time I find myself wondering if his hair is as soft as it was then. In an instant, my imagination runs wild, and I want to know how those strands feel when I curl my hands around his head as he moves his lips down my body. He brought me such highs with that mouth. That wickedly talented mouth.

Oh, dear heavenly dirty fantasy. I press my thighs together as a pulse beats between my legs.

"Your secret is safe with me," he says, lowering his voice, and for a moment I tense, thinking he knows who I am and can tell that I'm still turned on by him. Will he mock me for toying with him, or toss down his napkin and announce he never showed up that day because he never cared for me?

"My secret?" I ask nervously, cursing my body for having the audacity to be aroused this goddamn easily.

His voice drops further. "That you're the wine snob, Penny," he says, clearly joking, and I breathe again, a big, deep breath that relaxes me.

Laughing, I shake my head. "I swear I'm not a wine snob. I do, however, think wine is one of the three proof points that the world can indeed be a good place."

"And what are the other two?"

"Music and dogs," I answer. "Give me wine, music, and dogs, and I'm happy."

He furrows his brow. "But I thought dessert was one of your great loves. You did warn me in advance of tonight about your feelings for dessert."

"Oh." I bring a finger to my lips, tapping them. "It seems I've miscounted. Four things."

He takes my Tempranillo and holds it up. "To the four proof points of a good world."

I reach for the sangria and clink my glass to his, and I'm happy—not angry—that we're having a lovely time. Maybe I should be disturbed that I don't want to kick him in the balls. But my high-heeled feet are flat on the wood floor, and I have no inclination to inflict bodily harm on the man who broke my heart.

Perhaps the ice I thought had encased my heart when it came to this man is breaking.

Gabriel

When the waiter returns, we order our dinners. After he leaves, I turn my gaze to Penny, eager to know her better. Already, I like her for her. She's fiery, but sweet. Confident, like when she issued her decree on the flavors in the wine, but playful and teasing, too. She keeps me on my toes, makes me laugh, and intrigues me.

That's why following Tina's advice is easy. I slide right back into conversation without skipping a beat.

"Tell me more about how you came to work in the charitable field," I say, since I've always been curious how people find their way into their work. "Was it luck? Happenstance? Coincidence? Or a long and abiding love?"

"I love animals," she says, as if it's the easiest answer in the world.

"That's the best reason."

"Sometimes I think we try too hard to find the perfect field, the perfect job. We try to figure out the color of our parachute. But really, the answers are here," she says, tapping her heart.

I nod, agreeing wholly with her. "I believe that, too. When you're happy with what you do, it's because it comes from who you are."

She beams, and her smile is infectious, genuine, and it feels like sunshine. "Exactly. My grandmother said true happiness comes from what you do when it's aligned with your heart."

"Your grandmother is a wise woman. My mother used to say something similar. To do what you love," I say, then return to the topic of four-legged friends. "Since you love dogs, does that mean you have a dog?"

"I do. She's great. I'm crazy about her," she says, then she takes a drink. Her tone is sweet, almost as if she's keen to tell me more but unsure if I truly want to hear about her pet.

Setting one elbow on the table, I rest my chin in my palm. "Tell me about your canine friend."

"Her name is Shortcake," she says, a note of pride in her voice.

I smile. "That's adorable."

"Because she's little," she says, holding out her hands to show a small amount of space.

"And because you like dessert," I add as I reach for my glass, letting her know I've been listening.

"Strawberry shortcake is pretty damn good," she says, and her smile widens. Like that, she looks younger. Her light brown eyes sparkle, and the grin makes her seem almost...

I blink, momentarily transported to another place. I swear an image of Penelope slips over Penny, and the two seem one and the same. It's as if I'm in two lives at once—this one here with her, and a past life with a girl I was falling in love with in hardly any time at all. I don't know that I've ever believed in love at first sight, and that's not precisely what happened with the mystery woman from my past. But it was as close as I've ever come, because the last night with her, I knew I was falling. That was why what happened next was so goddamn miserable.

I straighten my shoulders, setting down the glass as I recall Tina's advice. I fight like hell to stay in this moment.

"Was it love at first sight?" I ask, and just to make sure I don't take a trip to a decade ago again, I add, "With your dog?"

Penny nods happily. "Shortcake insisted on being mine. When she came to the shelter, she stood on her hind legs, put her front paws on me, and wagged her tail. When I leaned down to say hello to her, she covered me in kisses."

"She's not one for beating around the bush, is she?"

"And it wasn't just her sales pitch, either, to get me to take her home," she says, radiating excitement. "She hasn't changed one bit. She's really like that. She's incredibly affectionate, and she kisses me all the time."

Before I can think better of it, I say, "And you like that? Being kissed all the time?"

This time, I'm thinking of *her*. The woman across from me.

Chapter Six

Penny

Perhaps the ice has already cracked. Maybe it happened when Delaney pointed out that Greta was likely the flirt, not Gabriel. Maybe it began to dissolve when I walked through the door tonight and saw him waiting for me—the image I'd longed for years ago. Or possibly, the ice is melting because this man across from me is a man I want to know. And to know again.

When he asks me about being kissed, my thoughts turn neon hot and electric.

And you like that? Being kissed all the time?

Fine, we're talking about my dog. But we're talking about *lips* and *kisses*. And no one has ever kissed me like Gabriel.

That day in Park Güell, when he breathed out *kiss me*, we became lost like that. Tangled up in each other, mouths searching, tongues finding, breath mingling.

"I could do this all day," he said.

"And all night?"

"If you want me to, there's nothing I'd rather do." His voice was laced with desire.

"I want you to kiss me," I said, boldness and desire overcoming me as I moved my mouth to his ear, whispering, "everywhere." We didn't stay in the park much longer. In fact, I think we set a land-speed record, grabbing the blanket and running to his room.

Somehow, I find the will to slam the blinds closed on that far-too-tantalizing memory, and try to remember what we were talking about before my mind ran loose. His job? Cooking? I'm not sure any longer, so I say, "Do you?"

He drums his fingers on the table. "Do I like being kissed?"

Oh God. My face flames red. I'm not even adding transitional thoughts anymore to my speech with him. I shake my head quickly, making a rolling gesture as if I'm cycling him back to the spot where I left off, though it was many moments ago when we'd talked about our jobs. "Do you love cooking?" I ask, the words coming out stilted because all I'm thinking about is kissing.

He laughs. "That was an interesting segue."

I glance at my hands. Run my finger along the stem of the wine glass. Fold and unfold my napkin.

Mercifully, he doesn't ask if I'm nervous or embarrassed. Though the answer is both, and I swear I'd like to grab a paper bag, drop it on my head, and have someone yank me away from the table. Smack some sense into me. Because this is the definition of foolish. I can't fall into Gabriel's orbit, and yet…that's what I'm doing.

"Just as you love animals, I love to cook," he says.

And there it is. An elegant simplicity to who we are. "That's the best reason to do what you do," I say, repeating his words because they ring true to me, too. "For love."

"I believe, too, that it is easy to be misguided," he says, pushing the cuff higher on his shirtsleeve. "To think maybe we want to do something else. But as you say, the answer is often here." He points to his breastbone. "Did you always know you wanted to work in philanthropy?"

"I thought I wanted to be a—" I stop myself before I say *banker*. I don't know if I'm ready to remove my armor yet. To reveal too much too soon. I swallow and correct myself. "I thought I wanted to work in business. But I knew after six months that it wasn't for me. And you? Has the love affair with food been a forever kind of thing?"

He laughs lightly. "I'm lucky in that regard. From the time I was a young boy, learning how to cook an egg at my mother's side, I knew the kitchen was my home."

A pang of guilt stabs me, because I remember him telling me about his parents, his sister, his brother, and how they grew up with very little and someday he hoped to give them more. A confession starts to well up inside me, to fight its way out soon. *When you asked me if we'd met, you were right. We did so much more than meet. Please tell me you remember everything like I do. And that you remember it fondly.*

And whether he does or not, I don't want to pretend to be someone else—someone unknown to him. I want our history, not just the present. Nor can I play this game much longer when he's being so open with me.

"Though I'm lucky in that regard, not in others," he adds, as the waiter brings the plates and sets down our food.

"Why do you say you're unlucky?" I ask, and now that guilt deepens because I can't help but wonder if something tragic prevented him from meeting me again. Something terribly sad. My throat hitches, but I swallow it down. I need to know. "Is your mother okay?"

"Oh yes. My family is all fine," he says, reassuring me as he thanks the waiter and I do the same. "I just meant there were things I wanted that didn't happen. Jobs that fell through."

"There were?" I ask, and a wave of relief rolls gently through me as we eat and talk.

He nods as he lifts his fork. "Yes. And I didn't take it well. I thought everything was supposed to happen how I wanted it to. But I have to remind myself that I'm lucky to have what I have now, and I try to give back to my family. To do what I can for them. If things had unfolded in a different way, perhaps I wouldn't be able to do that. I have to believe that we're on the path we're supposed to be on," he says, his delicious accent wafting over me, intoxicating me, along with his words of loyalty, and family, and the fickle finger of fate. "I have to believe in fate, too." He takes a beat, holding my gaze. "Do you? Believe in fate?"

Fate.

And like that, I tumble back in time.

"Do you believe we were meant to meet, my Penelope?" he asked the last night we were together, moonlight streaking across his warm skin through the open window in his room.

"I do," I said, breathless from the lovemaking, from the way he absently ran his finger along my hip, down my thigh, making me shiver even after he made me come again and again.

"I believe in it with you," he said, then he climbed over me, pinned my wrists above my head, and smothered my neck, my throat, my breasts in kisses, making me squirm in pleasure, making me moan with need. When he raised his face, his eyes full of lust, he dropped his lips to my mouth and kissed me madly. Then he whispered against my lips, "I will see you again. I have to."

A clattering of dishes from the kitchen snaps me back to the present. I set down my fork and bring a hand to my temple, pressing my fingertips hard against my head as if I can push away the dizzying reminders of all that we had, all that we wanted, all that we planned.

I meet his gaze, and his eyes seem so honest, so truthful, as he asks me about fate. Here with him, right now, I'm not sure how I could believe in anything else.

Even if it scares the hell out of me. I hate that I like him. I love that I like him.

Which one do I want to win out?

Love or hate?

But really, there's only one answer.

"I suppose I do believe in fate," I say, and a ribbon of warmth unfurls in me, flowing from head to toe. It feels delicious and mutinous at the same time, because it reminds me of how easy it was to fall under his spell, since it's happening again. I try to center my thoughts on my mission for being here with him tonight—to understand why he's an ex, not to serve up my whole truth.

Nicole had said that ex-boyfriends are in the rearview mirror for a reason.

For ten relentless years, Gabriel has been my benchmark. In that time, I've dated, I've fallen in love, I've nearly become engaged. But even so, a part of me has held back. A portion has been hobbled by fear—fear of being used. Stood up. Cast aside. Is there something unlovable in me? Is there some part of me that could make a man leave me standing all alone by a fountain again?

I'm not the dewy-eyed girl who fell for him at twenty-one. I'm older, wiser, and experienced enough in the world to know what I want—I want *the one*. And if I don't put what I had with Gabriel to rest, I'm not sure I can ever be in a place to have that.

How can I move forward if I'm still plagued with questions from the past?

After the waiter refills our drinks, I take the sangria and down a hearty gulp, seeking liquid courage.

Gabriel lifts the other glass and I watch him, all the sounds of the restaurant blending into a distant soundtrack as the voice in my mind rises above the rest. Like a chorus to a song, growing louder, the words repeat in my brain. *Tell him, tell him, tell him.*

He never takes his eyes off me. His gaze is intense, as if he's memorizing me. A flurry of nerves spreads inside me, but it's mixed with something else, too. A strange new hope that I can speak the truth and not reopen the wound. That I can say what I need to and not regret it.

But words slip through my fingers under his stare. His eyes darken, and I swear he roams his gaze over every inch of my body— my arms, my breasts, my neck, and even my hair. Then they linger on my shoulder, and they don't seem to stray from the flowers marked on me. My tattoos remind me of desire. They remind me of femininity. They remind me of strength. Of the girl who had the courage to spend a summer in Europe after college even when her parents didn't want her to. The girl who only knew enough Spanish to get by when she boarded the plane, but who learned enough in her travels to speak to nearly anyone. That girl was bold enough to talk to this man at a café on the streets of Barcelona.

And later, many months later, she was courageous enough to walk away from a job she didn't love and to take the leap into one she's still passionate about.

Maybe that strength was forged years ago when I was in Europe, or perhaps when he left me at the fountain.

"Those are absolutely beautiful," he says, staring at the deep pinks and rich purples on my skin. His voice is rough, like it was when he was kissing me, when he'd grow more and more turned on.

"Thank you," I whisper, my voice like a feather.

"How long have you had them?"

I raise my fingertips to the lily, tracing it. "The lily is new. Only a few months old. The others I had done several years ago." I swear I can hear a rumble in his throat, like a low, needy groan as I touch the ink. The way he stares is almost unabashed, as if he's not ashamed to look at me like this, with desire in his eyes. Because that's what I see.

There are no two ways about it.

I want him still.

And he wants me.

This me.

I don't know why it didn't register before. Maybe because I was still too shocked. Maybe I'm a fool with him. But this is a date. He asked me—Penny—on a date. He hasn't once talked about the event like he'd said he wanted to. He didn't ask me here to this romantic restaurant with its soft music and low lights to talk about work.

My heart speeds up, and the hair on my arms stands on end.

We haven't spoken of the picnic, or anything else but each other. And now he looks at me as if I'm the next serving of this meal.

The trouble is I don't know what to make of the fact that he asked me out. Does it affirm that he's a playboy who simply gobbles up women? Or does it mean I'm special? And is that what I want out of tonight? To be desired? For him to take this new me home? Or is it for him to know that I'm the same woman who fell for him and that I can't get him out of my mind years later?

The questions plague me, tugging my certainty in opposite directions. My bravado slinks away.

Soon enough, the waiter clears our plates, and when he leaves, I say thank you to Gabriel.

"No. Thank *you*," he says.

"For?"

"For having dinner with me." The sentiment sounds completely earnest. As far as I can tell, he's been honest with me the entire meal. I can't last much longer without telling the truth. I'm not this person. I want to be the kind of woman who is open and honest, even when I don't know the score. I have to be true to me.

"Dinner was amazing. All of it," I say, and that's the whole truth.

"But if memory serves, you said you're not satisfied until you have dessert."

Chapter Seven

Gabriel

As she eats the crème brûlée, that sense of déjà vu slams back into me, like a punishing wave. I try to keep my head above water and cling to the present, but I'm a man shuttled back and forth in time. I can't shake off the past.

I thought I'd succeeded, that I'd followed Tina's advice and gotten to know Penny for Penny, and I have. To be sure, Penny is completely captivating. She's hooked me, and I want to see her again, to talk to her again, to get to know her more.

But as these thoughts lead me on, I'm like a dog yanked behind by a leash. Someone is tugging me in the other direction.

Even as I try desperately to maintain my footing in the most wonderful first date I've had in ages, I can't hold on. I succumb to the wave, sinking under.

* * * *

I was taken with her the moment I sat down at the table next to hers at the café on a street corner in Barcelona. Her warm eyes met mine, and I wasn't able to look away, so I didn't. When her almond cake arrived, she arched an eyebrow, and said, "You're admiring my dessert."

I laughed. "I don't think it's the dessert I'm admiring. But I have been hoping you'd want company to help devour it. May I join you?"

She nodded and I moved to her table. She picked up her fork and said, "It's made with caramel—my favorite. And it's divine. By all means, let's devour."

"I'm a big believer in the consumption of sweets."

"We have a saying in America. Eat dessert first," she said.

I lifted my fork and took a bite of the Tarta de Santiago. "I like this saying. Can you appoint me a temporary American?"

She tapped my shoulder, something that shouldn't have turned me on, but somehow it did. "There. Done. By the power vested in me, I've declared you able to eat dessert first."

"I must tell you a secret. I already possessed the ability," I said, and she laughed, a pretty sound, like bells.

And I was halfway to hooked. Maybe it was her confidence. She seemed a few years younger than me, but there wasn't a shred of shyness or insecurity about her. Her wit was intoxicating, and so was her beauty.

When we finished the almond cake with the caramel layer on the bottom, I was certain of two things—I didn't want to let her get away, and I needed to see her again. "May I take you to dinner?" I asked.

She said yes.

But we didn't wait till dinner. We spent the afternoon together, wandering around the city, strolling through the side streets, ducking into the churches and buildings and seeing the sights she wanted to explore.

All the while, I learned more about her. That she'd studied European History in college, that she'd loved traveling across the continent these last few months, and that she was looking forward to her job on Wall Street at Smith and Holloway Bank when she returned to the United States.

Mostly, she added. She was mostly looking forward to it.

"This trip is my last hurrah before I enter the working world," she told me.

"Then let's make sure you make the most of your last few days here. Would you like that?"

"I would like that very much."

Then I kissed her in the moonlight and it felt like this was exactly why I was meant to work in Barcelona that summer. Later, when I told her I had a job in New York, I was more sure than ever that fate was looking out for me.

* * * *

"This is delicious crème brûlée, but what I really want to know is if yours is better," Penny says, as if she's throwing down the gauntlet.

"Of course mine is better. Is that your way of saying you want me to make one for you?" I say, wiggling an eyebrow. If she's going to flirt with me, then, hell, am I ever going to flirt right back.

"I would never turn down a dessert like this," she says, and I can picture her in my kitchen, cooking for her, bringing the spoon to her lips, saying *try this*.

She'd dart out her tongue, lick a dash of the delicious concoction, and roll her eyes in delight. Then she'd tell me what else she wanted to sample. I'd grab her hips, push her up against the counter, and show her that my skills extend all through the house, from the kitchen to the bedroom, and any place else she wants to try.

"Would you like to do this again, Penny?"

Her lips part, and she doesn't answer at first. She sets down her fork, spreads her hands over her napkin, then meets my gaze. "I would, but there's something I need to…"

"What is it?" I ask, wondering if there's an issue with us working together on the event, if she needs to wait until it's over for us to go out again.

"It's that—"

A male voice breaks the moment. "And how was everything?"

I grit my teeth but flash a smile at the waiter, though I wish he knew not to interrupt a conversation. "Everything was wonderful. We'll take the check," I say, and when he leaves I return my attention to Penny. That youthful vulnerability is back in her eyes.

It's knocking me off-kilter. I can barely focus on the moment, so I excuse myself for the men's room, splash water on my face, grab a paper towel, and pat my cheeks dry.

When I return, crossing through the tables, I stop in my tracks. Penny's back is to me for the first time. She fiddles with her hair. All those long, lush strands are up in her hands, her neck exposed.

A hush falls over my world, like the rest of Manhattan has gone mute, and the spotlight is only on her.

I know it's her.

I'm positive.

I've kissed that neck. Outside a dress shop in Barcelona, where I told her she'd look lovely in a red dress. I wrapped my arms around her from behind and dusted soft, tender kisses on the back of her neck, her feminine scent drifting into my nostrils. "You'd look so lovely in that, my Penelope. And even lovelier when I take it off you. Actually, just wear nothing with me."

She laughed and leaned into me, tilting up her face. "Maybe next time you see me, I'll be wearing that dress and you can have your wish."

"Having you again is my wish. Having you tonight is my wish right now."

"Have me," she whispered.

Time no longer slides jarringly back and forth. The two warring trains that kept crashing into each other on the same tracks are now linked together. Penny is my Penelope, and I'm struck with a sense of wonder. A feeling of awe. Scrubbing my hand over my jaw, I try to decide what to do next. And whether I should feel mad, thrilled, frustrated, or hoodwinked.

I'm sure she knows I'm the same person—same profession, same last name.

I'm not sure why she didn't tell me, but right now I want to hear her say it. Who she is to me. I want the words to fall from those lips I could never have kissed enough.

I walk up to her, filled with a deep desire that had gone latent over the years but has been reignited in an evening. Gently, I set my hands on her shoulders. She flinches, but softens immediately as she turns to meet my gaze. I bend my head to her neck, about to ask *"Did you ever get the red dress?"*

But she speaks up. "Gabriel, when I said there was something I needed to tell you, it's this—you were right. You've met me before."

The fact that she went first thrills me. "I know," I whisper, and she shivers as my breath ghosts over her neck. "You're my Penelope."

"I am." Her voice is filled with the same sort of hope that

courses through me. I can't help myself. I press my lips to her neck in the softest, barely there kiss. She trembles, and that's all I need to know. "I'm Penny Jones."

I reach into my wallet, fish around for some bills, and toss enough and then some on the table to cover the check.

I take her hand and lead her out of the restaurant. We walk a few feet away, stopping in front of a brownstone with a long, green set of steps, and a small iron fence running around the street-level front. A tree canopies us, and the road is blissfully quiet for now. The glow from a nearby streetlamp illuminates her face.

Her face.

I'm not crazy. I'm completely sane, and I knew it had to be her. Now I want to know what the hell is going on. "Why didn't you say who you were the other day?" I ask, and that small shred of frustration bubbles back up. "You said you were Penny Smith."

She shakes her head, biting her lip. When she exhales, she answers, "I wanted you to realize it was me. I didn't want to be the one to tell you. I wanted you to see me and know me in a heartbeat. Just like I knew it was you."

I grip her hand tighter, standing closer. "I knew it was you. My God, I knew it was you. Do you know how many times I looked around and wanted to see you?"

Her mouth falls open. Her eyes turn to moons. "No. I don't know that at all. How would I know?" she asks, full of disbelief. "You never showed up at Lincoln Center."

I drag my free hand through my hair and heave a frustrated sigh. "I'm well aware I didn't make it to New York ten years ago. But why wouldn't you say who you were now? The other day, sure, I suppose I can understand. But tonight? Not once?"

With her eyes narrowing, she hisses, "Because you should have recognized me. You should have known I was the same girl you slept with," she says, anger radiating off her. "I gave you my virginity, and you knew that. How could you sit across from me at your restaurant and not recognize me? Is it because you're Manhattan's sexiest chef? Or maybe because you were busy being the heartbreaker in the kitchen all these years after you ditched me?" She shimmies her shoulders, tossing off the nicknames like terrible insults. And her words sting. The names, which I never wanted but are far too true, are little stabs in my chest.

"Oh, I knew it was you. Trust me. I knew," I say, spitting out the words, annoyance getting the better of me. "I didn't forget you, Penelope."

She arches an eyebrow. "Really? Is there room in your memory for one more? Because you broke *my* heart, so the name fits."

"Stop," I say, holding up a hand before we veer too far in the wrong direction. "Stop saying those things. Don't punish me for what I did before you waltzed back into my life. Because as soon as you did, I asked if we'd met. How many times did I ask you? But then you flat-out denied we knew each other. You were certain. Adamant. And you said you were Penny Smith. I *chose* to believe the woman I'd just met rather than continue questioning her. And you don't look the same. Your hair is longer and darker, and your shoulder is covered in all those fucking gorgeous tattoos. Why shouldn't I have believed you when you said we'd never met?"

She raps her knuckles against my chest. "You should have known here. You made me feel stupid. You said you believed in fate. You said '*I will see you again. I have to.*' Those were practically your last words to me in Spain."

I grab that free hand from my chest and grip it, wrapping my palm over her tight fist. Both her hands are in mine, and I won't let her go. "I didn't ever want you to feel stupid. Not then. Not now. So, no more games. No more pretending—"

She jumps in, the vein in her neck beating hard as her pitch rises. "You want to know why I didn't say 'I'm your Penelope'? Because I waited for you, Gabriel. You promised you'd show. You said how much you wanted to see me again. I stood outside that fountain for two hours. *Hoping.* And you never emailed. I never heard from you. Not a peep. Not that day. Not the next. Not once through all the years. Do you have any idea how much that hurt?" Her voice breaks, as if she's a heartbeat away from tears. "Why would I think anything other than you got what you wanted from me in Barcelona and then didn't want to see me again?"

The sheen in her beautiful brown eyes tells me exactly how much it hurt. My actions didn't just wound her. They cut her deeply. "That was the last thing I ever wanted to happen," I say in a rush.

But my words hardly register as she raises her chin higher and pushes against my chest with our joined hands. For a moment, it occurs to me that she might run. I don't want her to escape, but I'm not the kind of a man who's going to force her to stay.

I let go of her hands. She doesn't slip away from me, though. Instead, she grips my shirt, fisting the fabric near my collar, her eyes blazing. "Then tonight you take me out and you romance me, and you make me realize why I fell for you in the first place. And I don't want to feel stupid again when you don't show up." A pair of tears slide down her cheeks, and her voice turns impossibly soft, but she doesn't look away. "Because it's happening again. I'm starting to fall for you all over again."

Cupping her shoulders, I lean in and kiss away one tear, then the other. "It is my greatest regret," I whisper against her soft cheek. "All I wanted was to see you again. I wanted it so much."

Her anger drifts away, like smoke. "Why didn't you show?"

Taking a breath, I back away to meet her gaze. "In retrospect, it's kind of a funny story."

Chapter Eight

Gabriel

She's wedged against the iron fence, and I'm inches away.

She waits for me to explain my absence, and she probably expects a tragedy. Something worthy of the movies. Or a Nicholas Sparks novel.

But there's no terrible misfortune here. No fire. No mother who hid handwritten letters. No horrific accident that prevented me from writing.

Just fate. Just life. Just a stupid mistake made by my twenty-four-year-old self in a fit of rampant frustration. I'm going to sound like an idiot when I tell her. But fuck, that's the cost. I blurt out, "I threw my phone."

She scowls, her eyes registering surprise. "You threw your phone?" she asks, like it will make more sense if she repeats it.

"Yes. And I know I should probably have some dramatic explanation, like my grandmother died, or my mother was taken ill, God forbid. But those aren't the reasons."

Her expression softens. "I'm glad they're okay. They are okay, right?"

I nod. "Yes, everyone is fine and good and ridiculously healthy. My sister is married and has twin boys. My brother is engaged. And my mother is retired from teaching now."

"Because of you?" she asks, tilting up her chin.

"Yes. Because of me. I take care of them now. But the point is," I say, pausing to take a breath, "I wanted to see you again more than nearly anything. I had the job in New York working at a restaurant. My cousin in Miami had connected me with the restaurant—it was run by his friend. And the morning you left, I found out my work visa was denied."

Her eyes widen. "Oh no."

I close my eyes briefly and pinch the bridge of my nose, recalling my frustration as I'd stared at the official government letter denying my application. Hot anger had seared my blood that morning a decade ago.

When I open my eyes, I tell her what I learned when I went to the mailbox in the building where I sublet my room. "You'd gotten on your plane, and I finally checked the mail. I don't think I checked it once when you were with me. I was…" My lips twitch, then I add, "otherwise occupied."

A smile tugs at her lips, too, and I continue.

"I opened the mailbox, and there was my *beautiful* letter from the government. I was sure it would be my visa. My permission to go to the States and work there. I even kissed the stupid envelope, thinking it contained all the good news in the world. I'd wanted the job badly. For the money and the opportunity, and then to see you. It seemed like a done deal," I say, desperation coloring my tone, just remembering that tense anticipation. "The people who ran the restaurant had assured me the visa would work out. They'd requested others for chefs that had gone through successfully, and they were sure they'd get one for me. I had the job, and they'd gotten plenty of other work visas approved without a problem. And at last, mine had arrived."

Her eyes cloud with sadness, and I reach for her hand again. This time, we link fingers, and it feels like magic and desire all at once. But there's so much more to say, so I keep going. "I rushed back up the steps to my crummy little studio, which was hardly crummy anymore because it was where I'd spent those nights with you, and I slid my finger under the seal and opened the letter." My shoulders sag. "Denied. Work visa denied. I was so fucking mad. And then I tried to call you."

She tilts her head, her eyebrows rising in question. "You did?"

"Of course," I say, confidently. "I called you before I called my cousin."

"I must have been on the plane," she says, her voice soft, as if she's tripping back in time, too. Then a new realization seems to hit her. "Oh God. Even if you left a message I would never have gotten it. All I had was that little temporary flip phone for traveling. And it stopped working as soon as I left the country."

"Exactly. Because everything was different ten years ago."

"We didn't have smart phones." It's as if we're both reminding each other of the different time in which we met. "You couldn't just live in New York and call a friend in Paris. Skype wasn't a thing we used regularly."

Penelope and I had exchanged cell numbers when we'd met so we could be in touch for those few days when she was in Spain. But her phone had been a temporary one, set up on a European carrier for local calls and emergencies.

"There was no way for me to call you once you left Spain," I say, but we weren't stupid. We'd planned for this when we'd exchanged emails and then picked a time and place in New York to meet. "You didn't have your new cell yet. You were going to buy one when you returned to the States. We'd talked about how by the time you were set back up in the U.S., I'd be there. Seeing you again." I choke out a bitter laugh at the sheer irony.

"I thought that, too," she says, looking at me from under her lashes. Her wide eyes are earnest now, and the anger that whipped through her minutes ago seems to have faded into the night. "But what about email? Why didn't you email me and tell me what happened with the job? I'd have understood."

"This is the part of the story that is funny, but only in retrospect," I say, taking a deep breath. "When I reached your voicemail, and it was just a recording saying *this number is no longer a working number*, or whatever it said, that only intensified my frustration. I didn't have the job. I wasn't going to the U.S. And I couldn't reach you to tell you, so I threw my phone against the wall."

She blinks and furrows her brow. "That's an intense reaction."

"I'm not a guy with a temper, Penelope. You have to know that, but I wanted to see you again so badly, and when I couldn't reach you I threw the phone."

"I've been known to toss a hairbrush at the wall myself. But does that mean you punished your phone since it couldn't reach *my* phone?" she asks, a note of playfulness returning to her voice.

"Yes. But I actually punished myself." I gulp and spit out the full magnitude of my stupid mistake. "Because your email was stored in the contacts in my phone."

"Oh God," she says with a gasp. Her eyes float closed, and she wobbles. I grip her hand tighter as she speaks softly. "That's why you never emailed me." She swallows, her lips quivering, then she opens her eyes. "And I didn't email you afterward because I was so upset when you didn't show."

I take her other hand in mine, holding both now. "I hated not being able to reach you. I half wish I could tell you I had your email on a piece of paper, and while I stirred a saucepan on the stove it fluttered out of my pocket, caught fire, and burned, and I desperately tried to save it, tossing buckets of water on the fire, but was left with only the charred remains of something at Hotmail."

A rueful smile tugs at her lips. "PenelopeJ5261 at Hotmail. It was the worst email address."

I laugh and nod. "That is the worst. You need to be Penelope at Gmail this time, please."

Her eyes shine with a new sort of happiness. "That sounds much better. But I'm PennyJones at Gmail."

I tap my temple and repeat her address. "Saved." I take a beat then return to the topic at hand. "But don't you see? I tried to tell you I wasn't coming. I wanted to email you. That was the only way I had to reach you then to tell you I wouldn't be making our date at Lincoln Center. My God, as soon as my phone hit the wall and clattered to the floor, I ran over, crouched down, and tried desperately to fix it," I say, the memory of my attempts to play phone technician flashing before my eyes. "Alas, telephone repair was never in my skill set. But you have to know, I hated that the job fell through, and more than that, I *hated* the thought of you going to the fountains to wait for me. It was like fate was laughing at me, and I hated that I couldn't see you or reach you. That whole day I thought about it. I pictured you. I saw you there, and it tore me up."

"Me, too," she whispers, and tears slip from her beautiful eyes again. This time, I don't kiss them away. I let her cry, because I sense she needs it. "I thought you stood me up."

"Of course you did. What else would you think?" I say, my voice gentle.

She swallows. "But you did try to reach me. You tried to tell me."

"I wanted desperately to reach you, to let you know I wasn't going to be there. That New York wasn't in the cards for me."

"Gabriel," she says, her voice like a confession. She lets go of my hands and places her palms on my chest. Her touch is electric and flares through my body. "I deleted your email a few days later. I threw out all your photos. I could have written to you, and I never did. I was so hurt when you didn't show, but I'm so, so sorry now."

I lean into her and dust a kiss on her forehead. "I'm sorry, too. I tried to call you at work."

"You did?" she asks, pulling back to look in my eyes.

I nod. "I remembered the name of your bank. Smith and Holloway. I found it through international information. I called when you were supposed to be starting, and the receptionist seemed a bit scattered."

Penny laughs. "She was. She was always mixing up messages." Then her mouth falls open. "Oh God. No. No. You left me a message at work, too?"

"I did," I say, and a surge of pride courses through me. Because now she knows how hard I worked to reach her.

She shakes her head. "It was like this running joke with the receptionist and her garbled messages. She quit shortly before I did. She hated it, too." Her expression shifts, as if she's remembering something else now. "Wait. You said something about throwing your phone on your reality show. I watched a clip a few days ago. You made a comment about it when you lost the salad hoedown or something?"

I groan. "Hey. There was no salad hoedown on the show. I would not have participated in a salad hoedown." I do tuck that name away—Salad Hoedown—since I want to tease Tina that it would make a good name for a band. "But yes, the producers asked if I was frustrated after losing a round of the bruschetta battle or whatever it was called. But losing that didn't come close to how pissed I was knowing I'd lost the way to contact you."

Soft fingers travel up the back of my neck. Then her hands are in my hair, and her lips are wonderfully near to mine as she says, "I'm sorry I said those things about you being the sexiest chef like it was a bad thing. I was hurt, and I lashed out. Forgive me?"

"There's nothing to forgive," I say, because her hands are on me again and all is right in the world.

She tosses me a seductive grin. "Besides, you *are* the sexiest chef, so can you just shut up and kiss me now?"

That I can do.

Raising a hand, I slide my thumb along her bottom lip, and she shudders. I'm done with words, done with talking. I only want to touch her again. Her lips part and her breath feathers over the pad of my thumb. It feels like anticipation. Like a deep and potent need.

She's the one who got away, and she's now returned. My lips brush hers, and the world stills. For the briefest second, I don't want to move. All I want is to savor this sliver of time—this most perfect of moments when I kiss her again.

For weeks, even months after she'd left, I longed for her. I'd asked myself how it was possible that we could spend only three days and nights together and yet I wanted her deep in my bones, far into the corners of my heart. As her lips seal against mine, and her fingers thread through my hair, the answer comes to me.

It arrives in the way I cup her jaw in one hand, in the glide of her mouth, soft and gentle over mine. It's self-evident in how she opens for me, her tongue darting out eagerly.

We fit, like we were meant to be.

Like we are the blueprint for kissing, handed down from on high. We are the lovers who make others jealous. We are the ones who connect so incredibly well that everyone wants what we have. I sensed it the day I met her. I felt it the first night I took her home. I was certain when I made love to her.

Penelope Jones drives me wild just by being her.

My free hand finds her hip, and I tug her against me, closing the remaining distance. Her slim body molds to mine, and that's more proof of *why* this woman captivated me from the second she walked into my restaurant the other day. Because my Penelope has been indelibly etched in my mind for ten years. Now, with her body angled to mine, my body remembers her.

She murmurs, and it's like a match to kindling. The sparks inside me roar as lust surges in my veins and, well, in other parts, too. I want her. I ache for her. My head spins, dizzy with desire that's lived through the years. Set on a low flickering flame, like a blue light, it's now hot and fiery once more.

Chapter Nine

Penny

My feet don't touch the ground. Gravity has no hold on me. I'm floating, falling, gliding.

My brain short-circuits as Gabriel kisses me, his lips both wonderfully familiar and fantastically new. My skin sizzles everywhere. Just *everywhere*. There's no part of me untouched by this kiss. It's consuming in every sense of the word. My mind is awash in endorphins, my heart hammers madly with happiness, and my body aches with an almost debilitating pleasure.

My fingers lace through his hair. And yes, his hair is softer than I remember. It's thick and lush, and I can't stop touching it. I can't stop kissing him. I don't want to break this connection now that we have it back.

I dreamed for so many nights of kissing him again, even as I fought against it. Still he visited me late at night in my fantasies. Hope was the cruelest torment, and it lasted so damn long.

And all those times I hoped, it was for *this*.

Him wanting me again.

He deepens the kiss, his lips claiming mine, his mouth owning me. Closeness is all I wish for, and he gives it to me, his lean, tall frame aligned to mine, his chest pressed to me, his erection hard as a rock against my hip. I'm barely aware of where I am, whether we're alone, if it's day or night. All I know is I want him to take me again, to have me, to make love to me.

I want him to strip me naked, kiss me all over, down my thighs to my knees, nipping my ankles, then back up again, settling between my legs.

I moan loudly into his mouth as my panties dampen. He swallows my sounds, and he's voracious, as hungry as an animal in the way he can't seem to stop kissing me. I think we might be as close to fucking as two people who are kissing can be. Quite possibly we've crossed some sort of line of public decency as I slam my body against his.

Thankfully it's New York, and no one cares that our arms and hands are tangled up in each other, or that I grind my hips against him, seeking his hard-on to fill the wild ache inside me. My body is empty and needy, and I'm dying for him to return me to the kind of ecstatic bliss I've only ever known with him.

He could fuck me here against this railing and I'd go along with it. I want him that much. I'm about to break the kiss and say *take me home now* when the faint sound of a dog's breathing reaches me through the haze of wanting.

My eyes flutter open in time to see an older woman walking a Papillon, and the sight snaps responsibility into focus.

"Shortcake," I say as I wrench apart from Gabriel.

"Hmmm?" His face is flushed and his eyes are dark and hazy.

"My dog. I need to go. To let her out and take her for a short walk. She's been alone for hours."

My comment seems to take a few seconds to register, then he nods. "Of course. I understand."

Somehow, we manage to separate from our fully-clothed almost-screw, and I smooth a hand over my shirt and then my hair.

"Penelope," he says, his voice low and smoky.

"Yes?"

"I'm not letting you go again." He licks his lips then, "Penny," as if he's adjusting to the name I use now.

A smile spreads on my face completely of its own accord. I think I might be the poster child for a grinning fool. "You're not?"

He shakes his head, his topaz eyes intense as he gazes at me. "No. Fucking. Way."

He takes my hand and gestures to the sidewalk. "I'm walking

you home. I'm kissing you again on the steps outside your apartment. And then I'm going to see you again tomorrow."

My smile is as wide as Manhattan. "Is that so? Is that like an order?"

He laughs as we walk. "Perhaps it is. Though I'm confident it's one we both like. But why don't you think of it more as a…" He stops, perhaps searching for the word. "A declaration of my intent."

Happiness floods my body and my brain. He always had a way with words. I squeeze his hand. "I accept your declaration, and I want it badly."

When we arrive at my building he does as promised, kissing me madly, deeply, truly. His lips travel up my neck, brushing the most tender kisses against my flesh until he whispers, "I want *you* badly. But Shortcake needs you. Can I join the two of you on your walk before I say good night? I would love to meet her."

And that's when I truly do swoon. He wants to meet my girl.

I run upstairs to leash her, and a minute later I return to him on the sidewalk. My seven-pound fur baby barks once at Gabriel, then decides to slather him in kisses when he bends down to say hello at her level.

"You are perfectly adorable," he says to my dog, and that warrants another swipe of her tongue against his cheek. "I can see why her sales pitch was effective."

We stroll through Manhattan, and as Shortcake sniffs the grass and trees on my block as if it were the first time she'd smelled them, we chat, starting to fill in the gaps of the last ten years. We talk about the restaurants he runs now, how he finally made his way to the United States a few years ago, starting in Miami where his cousin lives and opening his first restaurant there. He mentions his friendship with his business manager, who's French, too.

When it's my turn, I tell him how I started volunteering at a shelter, then writing grants, then eventually moved up to management. I mention Delaney and tell him that she's my closest friend and my fiercest ally, and he says he'll be sure to do everything in his power to never piss her off.

Then he thanks me for letting him join us on the walk.

If I hadn't already been falling for him at dinner, it's a done deal now. Especially when we return to the front of my building and he takes out his phone and taps out an email, speaking as he writes. "To Penny Jones at Gmail. Would you like to go out with me tomorrow night? Dinner? Rock climbing? Trapeze lesson? See a band and dance with me?" He raises his head and swipes his phone with a flourish. "Sent."

I grab mine from my purse, click on the new envelope icon, and hit reply. "Yes. The last one, please."

"Perfect answer," he says, then kisses me good-bye. Until tomorrow.

I float on a cloud all the way upstairs.

Chapter Ten

Penny

My sneakered feet pound the dirt path in Central Park.

"Told you."

The knowing comment comes from Nicole, part of my pack of running companions the next morning. By her side is Ruby, her Irish Setter mix. On her other side is Delaney, her blond hair swishing in a ponytail. Leading the pack is Shortcake, who trots ahead of us, since she's the fastest, most fearless one in the crew.

"What did you tell her, O Oracle of Relationship Wisdom?" Delaney asks as we round the top of the reservoir and the pale pink morning sun illuminates our way.

"It's the long-lost ring theory," Nicole says. "The same applies to Gabriel's thrown phone."

I give her a quick glance, arching a brow. "How so?"

"Well, the time I lost the ring," she begins, gripping her dog's leash tighter as a gray-haired man with a poodle approaches. "Ruby is a poodle-ist," she explains under her breath. "No idea why. Anyway, the time I lost my engagement ring from Greg, I freaked the hell out."

"Understandable," I say, as Shortcake pants and stares at the black-haired dog passing by. Shortcake is not a poodle-ist. "Losing a ring is one of the few acceptable reasons for freaking the hell out, along with finding your first gray hair and getting your period during a spin class." Then I add, "Incidentally, I don't have any gray hairs. But I plan to freak out when I do."

Delaney raises her palm and smacks it to mine. "Right there with you. But then I'm marching to the salon and having my stylist color it stat."

"There I was, freaking out," Nicole continues, "and I was racing through excuses and things I could say to Greg."

"Your possible options were…?"

"First, I planned to tell him I was giving a burrito to a homeless man, and the ring slipped off and fell into his cup."

"And then you remembered you don't eat burritos?" Delaney says, nudging Nicole.

Nicole laughs and taps her nose. "Exactly. My second choice was to tell him I lost it at the pool when I went for a swim at the gym."

It's my turn to chime in and debunk her. "And then you remembered you don't believe in swimming for exercise, only for relaxation, and it has to be in an infinity pool, preferably overlooking the cliffs of Los Cabos."

"You got it," Nicole says. "And finally, I toyed with telling him I was robbed. That someone broke into my apartment and stole it."

"And in the end, you didn't do any of those, right?" I say as we slow our pace, nearing the end of this morning's route.

"Exactly. Because the truth is it slipped down the drain. And sometimes when we try to concoct dramatic stories of what went wrong, they sound more ridiculous than the truth."

With my breath still coming fast, and a bead of sweat dripping down inside my sports bra, I turn to my friends. "And you're saying that means what? Because if memory serves, after the missing ring thing, didn't you ultimately decide it was a sign you weren't meant to marry him and called off the engagement?"

"I did," Nicole says, as we segue into walking. "It wasn't meant to be. And that's why I believe fate sent the ring down the drain."

"Does that mean fate made Gabriel break his phone?"

Nicole nods. "Exactly. The truth is messy and yet often simple. The dog doesn't eat the homework. We forget to do our homework. Or our ring slips down the drain. Or we chuck our phone at the wall because we're so goddamn worked up that we won't get to go to America and see the one we fell for," she says, giving me a knowing look.

"And is that fate or the truth?"

"Maybe it's one and the same," Delaney offers. "Maybe it was fate that you weren't supposed to see him again then, and just as fate took the form of a lost ring one day for Nicole, it became a broken phone for you and Gabriel."

"Does that mean his broken phone plus mine that no longer worked were the signs we weren't meant to meet again then...or also now? Or does that mean fate has taken the form of a picnic in the park this time around, with no other restaurant available but his?"

Delaney's lips quirk up. "I guess it's up to you to find out if he's back in your life for a reason."

* * * *

Tonight is for red wine and dark corners.

With red velvet curtains lining the walls, and dark, smoky lighting, the club in SoHo where the band plays is sultry and seductive. The musicians are magnetic, and the lead singer's voice could melt chocolate. The name cracks me up, though—Pizza for Breakfast.

"How did you hear about them?" I ask Gabriel during a short break in between sets. His hands have been on me all night. On my waist. Along my arms. In my hair. Have I mentioned this hands-on tactic of his has me all worked up? It's as if the dial has been switched to high, and I'm buzzed from his touch.

"My neighbor loves them," he answers. "She used to play cello for symphonies around the world, and now she's one of those people who finds cool new music."

"She sounds like my kind of person. Because I'm loving these guys." I finish the last of my wine and stretch my arm to the bar to set the glass down.

Gabriel slinks his arm tighter around my shoulders and tugs me closer. "Two out of three tonight isn't bad."

I arch an eyebrow. "Two out of three what?"

"Your favorite things. Wine, music, and dogs." He pauses, then adds. "But let's not forget your extra one. Dessert."

Tingles swoop from my chest down my belly, like a comet flashing across the night sky, simply because he listened. Because he remembered. "Maybe I'll have dessert later. Now, if this club would just have puppies for cuddling, the Den would be perfect," I joke.

He laughs. "We'll have to tell management your idea."

He drops a quick kiss on my neck that makes me shudder. I angle my face so our mouths meet, whispering *more,* before I brush my lips across his. He murmurs softly, and that sound turns into a low rumble I can feel in his chest as I deepen the kiss. A thrill streaks through me, and this time it comes from his reaction. From knowing that I've done this to him.

In some ways it feels like no time has passed with Gabriel. Here we are again, wrapped up in each other. The physical part is as easy as it was when we first met, the chemistry as electric and instant as the first day.

And yet, a decade has come between us, and as much as I want to spend the night getting more hands-on, I want to know this man better too.

Somehow I manage to break the kiss, and he lets out a playful whimper. "That was terribly unfair to tease me like that," he says, running his hands down my arms and setting them on my hips.

"Tell me your three things," I say, tapping his chest. "Your proof points that the world can be a happy place."

"Let's see," he begins, staring at the ceiling, and his accent thickens. It makes me wonder if he thinks in Portuguese, or if he maybe dreams in that language or another. If his mind reverts to the first languages he heard and spoke when he's deep in thought or sinking far into pleasure. That makes me wonder, too, if he still comes in French, like he did before. It was quite possibly one of the hottest things about him, how he'd moan and groan dirty words in his native tongue when he neared the edge. I brush aside my naughty thoughts to listen to his response as he meets my eyes again. "First, I would have to say beautiful tattoos."

"Yours are beautiful. You have new ones on your arms," I say, running my fingers along his ink-covered forearm. Then I drag my fingertip across a dark black line. "This tribal band? When did you get it?"

"Several years ago. It means family."

I smile softly. "Perfect," I say, thinking of how he supports his parents now. "I think it's incredible that you can take care of your family."

"It's a gift. I'm lucky to be able to do so."

"And this one?" I outline a circular design.

"The sun. For destiny. I had it done shortly after you left. It was my reminder to stay focused. That even when things were falling apart, I needed to still believe in my future."

"You had faith."

"I did. In many things."

"Okay, we've got beautiful tattoos. What are your other proof points?" I say, returning to the question.

"The second one would have to be traveling to new places. Exploring new towns or cities. Getting to know a culture or a people."

It's as if he's speaking my language, because I love those, too. "Yes. It's such a rush, isn't it?"

"Completely." He takes a deep breath. "And let's see. A third thing..." He tilts his head, as if he's studying me. When he raises his right hand to softly brush my hair from my face, it feels as if he's finding the answer in me. His voice drops lower, his gaze full of intent. "Your eyes."

"Oh stop," I say, blushing as my skin sizzles from his sweet words.

"You don't mean that, Penny. You don't actually want me to stop." He never breaks his intense stare, and it feels like everyone around us has faded to the shadows, like the spotlight of the night illuminates only us.

I shake my head and answer breathily, "No, I don't mean that at all."

His grip on my hip tightens, and he runs his thumb along my jawline. Inching closer, he angles his body to mine, his erection outlined deliciously against my jeans. "Gabriel," I whisper in a thin groan.

"What is it, Penny?"

"I feel like we're about to—"

A reverberation cuts through the packed club, and I snap my eyes toward the low stage. The singer clears his throat and speaks into the mic. "Hey there. Thanks for coming out tonight. We've got a new song we want to share with you, since you've been a great crowd. This one's a little slower, though."

As the guitarist plays the first chord, I tilt my face up to my date. "Dance with me."

"I thought you'd never ask."

We move a few feet to the crowded dance floor, and I wrap my arms around his neck. He loops his hands above my ass. Then he squeezes one cheek.

I gasp.

"And what was it you were about to say before? *I feel like we're about to...*" he hints playfully as the singer launches into a ballad-y number.

I arch an eyebrow. "You know what I was going to say."

He shakes his head as we sway. We're so close, so connected. My bones vibrate with desire for him. "No, tell me."

"It's just that being with you like this feels almost indecent."

He grinds his pelvis against mine, his thick cock so hard through his clothes. "*Almost* indecent?" he asks, arching his brow in a challenging stare. "Only almost?"

Heat races through me, rushing between my legs where I ache for him. "Fine," I huff. "It's indecent how hard you are and how wet I am," I say, and his eyes widen, as if I've shocked him by being bold.

A growl seems to emanate from him as he eases in closer. "It's indecent how much I want to fuck you right now," he rasps.

And I go up in flames.

I love that he says *fuck*.

Because right now, that's what I need.

We dance like that, pressed together, grinding, moving, rubbing, in the midst of all other bodies. I'm keenly aware of all of him—the heat from his skin, the scratch of his stubble, the steely press of his erection. The complete and utter lust for me that's identical to mine for him.

Sure, a decade has passed. Maybe we've both changed and grown. But some things remain the same. The chemistry that ignited us in Barcelona is even more powerful ten years later in New York.

"What's really indecent, though, is how much I'm going to torment you," he says with a fiery glint in his eyes.

"Why would you torture me?" With his hard-on rubbing against me in the middle of a goddamn club, I can't think. I don't want to think ever again. I want to feel everything with him.

He dips his mouth to my neck, dusting a kiss on the hollow of my throat that makes me squirm. Then he kisses his way up the column of my neck, and I'm not sure I'll ever recover from this kind of adoration. Nor do I want to.

"Because," he growls. "I want you to know that you're worth waiting for."

I tense as the full weight of his words settles on me. He wants to prove himself to me, which is a sentiment I love in theory. In practice, my body is shouting *take me now*.

"You're terrible," I say.

His eyes twinkle with mischief. "I know. But it won't be terrible in a few minutes."

Grabbing my hand, he tugs me off the dance floor and down the hallway. The music grows fainter as we round a corner, and he opens a restroom door. Once inside, I glance around. It's a single cubicle, one of those club bathrooms designed for dirty deeds. Dark and sexy, with black tiles and blue lighting, it screams "fuck me now."

He locks the door and pushes me to the wall, caging me in. I love his roughness. He was gentler in Barcelona. Now, the kid gloves are off. I'm not a virgin anymore, and I crave the manhandling from him.

One hand slides up my waist, over my breast, then behind my head, making me tremble as he moves along my body. He curls his palm around the back of my head, gripping my skull. "So, you're indecent, Penny?" he asks as his other hand plays with the hem of my shirt. The tremble turns into a long, sustained shudder as his fingers brush under the fabric.

"So indecent," I moan, jutting out my hips.

"Let's see how much," he says, running his finger over the button on my jeans.

I hitch a breath as his fingers play with me, as he toys with the button. My heart pounds relentlessly in my chest. Desire climbs up my legs, curling and twisting. It coils impossibly tighter as he slides open the zipper. God, I think I might come just from how he undresses me.

That's a thought I shouldn't keep to myself, so I say it aloud. "I think I might come from the way you undress me."

He groans, and his lips curve into a wicked grin. "I've barely started."

"Then please don't stop."

"Never," he says, his voice rough and demanding, and I was right about his accent. It's stronger in this moment, as if instinct shuts down rational thought. We are carnal creatures now, all heat and lust and craving.

His fingers dip inside my jeans, sliding over the outside of my panties, easing, toying, playing. He's not even between my legs and I think I might die if he doesn't touch me where I want him.

"Touch me," I plead, thrusting my hips, grabbing his shoulders. "I'm begging you."

He drops a tender kiss to my lips. "You'll never have to beg me. I always want to fuck you."

"But you said you were making me wait."

As his hand slides between my legs, his fingers slipping over the wet panel of my panties, he growls, "I have other ways to fuck you."

Lust consumes me. It cocoons me. It wraps me up, and this is all I am—the fevered wish to come. "Fuck me with your fingers." I'm absolutely pleading and I'm fine with it. "I need you so much. Please."

At last, he puts me out of my exquisite misery, and I whimper as he slides his fingers across me. "Oh God. Oh my God."

His shoulders shudder, and he pushes closer to me, his lean body pressed against my side as his fingers find a fast and glorious rhythm, sliding across all my slippery wetness, seeking my swollen bundle of nerves then driving me wild.

My eyes squeeze shut, and my body burns white-hot. My vision blurs, and it's as if I'm buzzing with electricity.

Noises and wild sounds fall from my lips. And from his, too.

Yes, please. So hot. Come for me.

He doesn't have to ask twice for that.

I'm nearly there. I was on the edge back on the dance floor. I was hovering when he pushed me to the wall. Now I'm climbing up that last cliff. As his finger flies over my clit, he thrusts another inside me, and I dip down on his hand, seeking more friction. I'm so far gone I barely know where I am anymore. My knees buckle, and he grips me tighter so I don't fall. In seconds, all the rapturous sensations twist inside me, and I shatter.

I break, falling apart into pieces of beautiful, lovely bliss.

I'm not quiet.

I cry, and I moan, and I sing out his name, and that hand behind my head clamps down on my mouth, covering up my loudest cries. Ripples of pleasure flood every corner of my body. I pant and I moan, and when I somehow find the ability to open my eyes again, he's grinning at me like he has a naughty secret.

He lets go of my mouth.

"What?" I ask.

"You're even more beautiful than I remembered."

"I am?"

He nods. "Yes, but especially when you come."

I smile dopily. "Guess I got to have dessert tonight after all."

He grins. "Three out of four then."

Then I reach for him. But when I rub my palm over his erection and say, "Let me," he shakes his head.

"No. I want to torment both of us."

And when I go home that night, I want him more than I ever did before.

Chapter Eleven

Gabriel

The next night we go to the Museum of Modern Art. As we wander through the paintings, we talk about the places we've been and what's to come.

"Tell me where you want to go when you explore the world again," I say as we stop in front of a Magritte.

She nibbles on the corner of her lip, not answering right away. Then she says, "Kyoto, to see all the temples. Prague, because it sounds like a city of fairy tales. And the Maldives, for when I want to be someplace where I can't be found."

I file away her answers, storing them safely in the drawers in my mind, which have now been reopened to her. It's as if I've stumbled upon a photo album that I once thought lost for good, only now there are new pages, new pictures, new memories to make. "Are you trying to escape from the world, Penny?"

She shakes her head as we round the corner. "Not lately. But if I wanted to escape, I'd want to be in one of those idyllic huts over the water," she says, sweeping her arm out wide. Her eyes sparkle as she talks. "You know the kind?"

I nod, picturing a trip to a faraway island. "Where the water is crystal clear, and the sand is like sugar, and the sky stretches in an endless expanse of blue."

She sighs contentedly. "Yes. That. Take me there."

I loop an arm around her waist. "I'd take you anywhere."

And then I kiss her, deep and hard, in front of a Kandinsky. She tastes like caramel and memories and all my dirty dreams.

When the security guard standing in the corner clears his throat, we move along, snickering as we go. "Too bad this isn't a sculpture museum. I'd tug you behind some huge statue and have my wicked way with you."

She tsk-tsks me. "Defiling a noble institution of art as part of your torment plan. I'm shocked."

"We were always quite accomplished at PDA, if memory serves," I say, running my hand along her spine as we stroll through another gallery. "Remember Papabubble?"

She stops and cocks her head, seeming to slide back in time. Then her eyes widen. "The caramel shop. Oh my God, the caramel shop."

"You loved caramel. You said it was your favorite."

"It is." She drops her voice to a whisper, angling closer to me. "You practically had your hand in my skirt while they were making candy behind the counter."

"Practically?" I say, acting offended at her recounting of the time I circled my hands around her waist, and then lower still, during our visit to the artisanal caramel shop in Barcelona. "I'm pretty sure it was *actually*."

A faint blush sweeps over her cheeks. "Only for a moment. I couldn't last like that in public. I swatted your hand away."

I hold mine up in surrender. "That made me so sad."

"Maybe that's why you pounced on me when we got back to your room."

"Your lips tasted like caramel, and you looked like the sweetest sin. How could I not?"

Her eyes dance with naughtiness as she moves closer in a sexy challenge. "And now? How do I taste?"

"I'd like to find—"

But I cut myself off when a mother marches into the gallery with two redheaded grade-schoolers in tow. Penny straightens and points her thumb at a red-and-black-splashed canvas. "Jackson Pollock. Overrated? Underrated?"

Bringing my hand to my chest, I feign humility. "I am but a lowly chef. How can I judge an artist like him?"

She scoffs. "Lowly chef, my butt."

Not covertly, I peek at her ass. "It is a lovely ass," I say when the trio is out of earshot. "Have I mentioned that?"

"No. Feel free to sing its praises," she says, then reaches for my hand. "By the way, I don't think you're a lowly chef. From what I've read, you're quite a superstar, and from what you made for me the other day, I'd say all the accolades fit."

I squeeze her fingers. "Thank you. Maybe you'll let me cook for you. Just you."

"*Let* you?" She arches a brow. "How about I demand you cook for me?"

"I'd love to." Then I circle back to something she said the other night. Calling me a playboy chef. "Do the other names bother you? The things that have been said about me?"

She exhales as if she's considering it. "At first, yes. But not anymore. I'm really trying to just focus on the here and now with you and me. Not what happened in between then and now."

"Not anymore? Are you sure?"

She nods, resolute. "Yes. I'm sure." I hope she means it. The other night she flung those words at me like insults. I understood she was hurt, and I'd probably have done the same if I were her. Even so, I want what's happening between us to be about *us*.

"I'm doing the same." I tap my temple and wink. "Besides, my brain has played this fantastic trick on me. It blots out any thought of what you've been doing from the moment you left Barcelona until you walked into my restaurant the other day."

She laughs. "Nice trick."

"It is. It's like this complete blankness. I love it," I say, because I hate the thought that any other guy has had his hands on her. I'm not a jealous man by nature, but the mere possibility that anyone else has ever touched this woman inflames me. It's not realistic to think she's been a nun for ten years, but I vastly prefer pretending I'm the only one who's been with her, ever.

Yes, that probably makes me a dick.

Perhaps I am on this count.

She shakes her head, bemused. "Yes, Gabriel. I'm as pure as the driven snow. Just like the day I met you."

"Perfect answer," I say, then I drop a quick kiss on the tip of her nose.

After we spend far too many minutes kissing in front of a Matisse painting of a goldfish, we decide it's best to take our brand of PDA out of the museum. We leave and get into the long, sleek car I had waiting for us at the curb. The driver pulls away, and before he slides up the partition I tell him to just drive.

"Speaking of taste…can I torture you now?" she asks, and I'd be a fool to deny her request.

"I believe I'm amenable to your brand of torture."

Soon enough she's unzipped my jeans and taken me into her mouth, and I'm not ashamed to say it hardly takes me any time at all because she looks like a goddess.

My goddess.

My beautiful woman with her long hair spilled over my thighs, and her red lips wrapped around my hard length. My hands cradle her head, and I guide her up and down, telling her how fucking good it feels the whole time. I groan as I stare at her, her head bobbing between my legs. Her tongue is divine. Her mouth is heavenly. And when she drags her teeth the slightest bit along my shaft, the angels of blow jobs weep with approval.

Because holy fucking heaven, Penny goes down on me like she loves it, and God knows I love the sight of her, the feel of her, the smell of her. And especially the passion of her—how much she seems to want to do this. She moans as she moves along my cock, and she makes such beautiful sounds—her murmurs, her groans, her noises of pleasure as she sucks me off.

My breath hitches and pleasure burrows deep into my body. Then, the desire grows more intense, more wild, more furious. My hands grip her tighter, clutching her head as I fuck her beautiful mouth.

Penny and I were never short on passion when we first met. We couldn't keep our hands off each other. I still can't get enough of her, but I also find we're freer this time around. She never went down on me like this before. She was younger, more exploratory. Now, she's wilder and hungrier, and it's fucking alluring.

I groan her name as I stare at her greedy mouth, stretched wide with my cock.

So fucking good.

So fucking hot.

You.

My God, you.

My thoughts turn baser and my words are no longer English. Soon, they're no longer words, just grunts and growls and noises as Penny licks and sucks me into a state of divine fucking ecstasy.

When I come in her mouth, my orgasm barrels through me, torching my blood and radiating in my bones.

Not just because she gave me an epic blow job. Because *she* gave it to me. This woman captivated me once, and she's done it again.

I am so far gone with her, and I don't want to ever turn back.

* * * *

Tina's raised eyebrow tells me she doesn't believe me.

As I slide the fresh basil to her and point to it with the knife, I defend myself once more. "Of course I have no problem giving up other women," I say, incredulous she'd suggest otherwise.

"You say that now…"

"Seriously. Why do you doubt me? Just because I'm a big fan of women doesn't mean I'm incapable of being with just *one* woman."

As she slides the blade over the leaves, she says, "The whole ladies' man persona is part of your identity. Not just as a man, but as a chef."

"Where do you come up with such insanity? Do I need to cancel the rest of your cooking tutorials for uttering such blasphemy?"

"You'd never do that to me," she says firmly, setting down the knife and pinning me with a daring look in her wise eyes. "Who else would be this blunt with you?"

I laugh. "Fine. You're lovely and blunt. But what is this nonsense about my identity?"

Her voice softens. "Your star rose right along with your popularity with the female sex. You've said it yourself. Perhaps not in those exact terms, but it wasn't hard to figure out. As soon as you were on that show and your restaurants grew more popular, the women flocked to you in droves."

She's not wrong when she says women and success have gone hand in hand. Yes, it's true that perhaps my rise as a chef paralleled a jump in attention from the press when it came to my dating, and an increase in my exploits, and a lot more women. "And that means…what exactly?"

"That your affection for women isn't just about women. I think a part of you believes your success is tied to the entire persona the show crafted for you. They molded you as the sexiest chef. And the question is this—once you're attached, can you still wear that crown?"

I scoff, dismissing her idea. Cooking is my love, and if I didn't believe in my deepest heart of hearts that I was meant to do it, single, married, or otherwise, I wouldn't have slaved over a burner and a skillet and a kettle for countless hours. "I love the theory, but the fact is, even if my professional and social identities have been intertwined, I have enough faith in my abilities to know the customers will show up regardless."

"Good."

"Besides, the past is the past, right?"

She answers me with a smile.

It better be. The past really better be behind us.

Chapter Twelve

Penny

Later that week, I head downtown to Gabriel's restaurant. When I turn onto Christopher, I spot the red wooden sign hanging above the door like a beacon. Funny how a little more than a week ago, I marched down this street, steeling myself, unsure what to expect. My armor strapped on, I was girded for battle.

Then, I was thrown for a loop when he didn't appear to recognize me.

Now, as I walk to his eatery to finalize plans for the event this coming weekend, a mix of confidence and happiness surges in me. It's such a welcome change from the last time I was here. When I press my palm on the glass door, I enter as the woman he wants, the woman he can't let get away.

But something in me seizes up when I see a mane of blond hair and hear a woman laugh.

"Wait till you try the blackberries, though. You'll be making a blackberry cobbler tonight for sure," she says, her voice like a cat's purr.

Tension flares in me when my eyes settle on the back of Greta's head and her long curtain of hair. She's chatting at the bar with Gabriel. The restaurant is quiet now, since it's not yet lunchtime. A swoop of dark hair falls over his eyes, and for a moment I picture her reaching out a hand, as if she's going to brush it away for him.

Jealousy burns white-hot in my blood. A fantasy unfurls, one of leaping onto her back, grappling her hair, and scratching her eyes out.

"I do enjoy a delicious blackberry cobbler," he says to her, and that's when I should launch my attack. Go airborne. Full woman-on-woman ambush. I rise up on my toes, and if I've got the angle right, I can fling myself on her, tackle her to the ground, and claw her away from my man.

But that's not what happens next.

Because what happens next has nothing to do with her or with him.

It has to do with me.

Taking a breath, I shoo away my errant thoughts.

I trust Gabriel, but more than that, I trust myself. There was a time when I doubted what I deserved in life, when I wondered if I was unlovable because he'd stood me up. But over the years, I made choices and I made changes. I sought out the kind of life I wanted to live. Yes, I'd been hurt when he didn't show. Deeply, terribly wounded. And for a long time, I'd shut down. Maybe I didn't let myself fall too far or too deeply for anyone else.

And I'd believed I was protecting myself from hurt.

But I know now that's not the reason I never fell for another man.

As I look at Gabriel, my heart thumping with a wild madness, the reason is this—my heart was given to him long ago.

And now, he has it fully—because of me and the choices I'm making this time around. To trust him. To believe in us. To have faith that he's with me.

I choose to believe that even if she flirts with him, it doesn't change who he wants.

He still wants me.

And I want him.

Even if he makes a comment about blackberry cobbler, he's not going home with her tonight. He's taking me to his bed.

And I don't care who he's been with before, or in between, or how many women have wanted the "sexiest chef." When he glances away from the produce purveyor and his eyes meet mine, they light up in a way that rocks my world.

There's no past that can come between what was meant to be.

Us.

His amber eyes shimmer with happiness when he sees me. They

don't just light the room—they power the whole city. I'm the one he's making dessert for.

With a grin I can't hide, I walk up to him, say hello, then extend a hand to Greta. "I'm Penny Jones. I run Little Friends. Nice to meet you."

A smile lifts on her pretty face. "Oh my God. I have a dog from Little Friends. A tiny little Min Pin who is a complete lapdog prince. So good to meet you."

My smile might now match hers. "I'm glad to hear that. What's his name? What's he like?"

Greta pulls out her phone from her pocket and proceeds to show me a photo of her little dude, reclined on a chenille throw with his paws crossed elegantly. She says she calls him Prince Harry, since she always had a thing for Princess Diana's second son.

"Perfect name for him," I say, as I mime stroking his chin on the phone photo. She laughs and then coos at her boy.

Gabriel wraps his arm around me and brushes a quick kiss to my cheek, murmuring something soft and sexy in my ear. Then he turns to the other woman while gesturing to me. "Greta, Penny is the woman I was telling you about yesterday. The one who got away. The one I once thought I lost."

Greta beams. "Seems she's been found."

Gabriel grips me tighter. "And I couldn't be happier. Especially since I think she'll like the dessert I have on the menu tonight when she comes over for dinner."

My heart does a jig. "I can't wait," I say, my voice a little breathy.

Greta pats Gabriel's shoulder, then slides in closer to give me a hug. That's when it hits me—she's just one of those people who likes to touch. Who likes to talk. I'd invented all those worries I had after the first time I met her. I'd crafted a story for her that was solely my imagination, fueled by my doubts from the past. Those doubts have been put to rest, and the reality is that Greta is a lovely person.

"You two are too sweet for me," Greta says. "I better go before all this swooning makes me go soft."

Then she winks and leaves, and I'm glad I chose not to be angry when I walked in. I chose to trust Gabriel before I knew Greta was so lovely.

But I don't want to think about other women any longer. I want to talk about me. I jut up a shoulder and meet his gaze. "So, I'm the one who got away?"

He answers me by slamming his mouth to mine, then whispering *yes* when we come up for air.

Somehow, we manage to finish our Picnic-in-the-Park planning, and the rest of the afternoon I daydream about blackberry cobbler and tonight and him.

I call Delaney and ask her to watch Shortcake this evening. I have a feeling I won't be coming home.

Chapter Thirteen

Gabriel

"I made you—"

I blink when I open the door and take in the sight of Penny. A black sleeveless tank with the thinnest straps I've ever seen hangs seductively on her. It shows off the art on her body. Flowers and vines travel across her flesh in dark pinks and deep purples. Her hair is pinned on one side again, and it's something of her signature look...with me, at least.

Tight jeans and black heels complete the outfit, and as I drink in the woman on my doorstep, my arousal kicks into top gear.

"Paella," I scratch out, finally finishing the sentence. "I made you paella."

She thrusts a bottle of Albariño at me and shakes her head.

I furrow my brow as I take the white wine. "I thought it was your favorite? You loved it in Spain."

"I do love it," she says, tiptoeing her fingers up my chest. "But I can wait to eat."

"And that means you can't wait for something else?"

One fist darts out, grabbing my black shirt. "No," she says in a hiss. "You've tortured me long enough. End it now, Gabriel. Please put me out of my misery."

Taking the wine, I put it in the fridge then turn off the stove. The pots can simmer. The dishes can keep. The wine glasses will have to wait to be filled.

"I hate the thought of you being miserable, my love." I take her hand and draw her close to me. Her body seals to mine, and in no time we're smashed together, two lovers tangled into one. We're limbs, clothes, skin, and a desperate need to be close, and then closer still.

This woman.

My God.

My brain fills with static. My head is hazy. I'm in the fucking clouds with her.

In some ways, I want to understand why I feel like this with Penny, and yet I don't ever want to know how we pull off this trick. Because it's magic, the way we are together. And if there's any secret to how we fit, maybe it's as simple as chemistry plus desire, as lust plus passion equaling two people who couldn't be more perfect for each other.

She's made for me, I'm certain. Penny is it for me. She's the beginning and the end, and what started with a spark has become a fire that will never burn out in my heart, mind, or body.

We break the kiss, and my breath comes in a harsh pant. "Come with me," I say, taking her hand and leading her to my bedroom.

When we reach it, I back up to the bed, sit on the edge of the navy blue comforter, and bring her between my legs. She stands. Setting my hands on her hips, I push up her shirt and press a hot, open-mouthed kiss to her navel. She trembles, and the taste of her skin intoxicates me.

I inhale deeply, wanting, needing, craving her scent in my nostrils, bathing my brain in the bliss that is her.

When I look up, she's shivering. I rise and cup her cheeks. "I need you to know something."

"What is it?"

My eyes never waver from hers. "There are a million ways I want to fuck you," I tell her, and her lips part. "I want to bend you over the bed, I want to put you on all fours, and I want to slam you against the wall and hook your legs around my waist."

"Oh God," she murmurs.

"I want to fuck you on a balcony with the New York skyline behind us. On the kitchen counter as your favorite band plays. I want to bring you down hard on my cock in the backseat of a limo as I fuck you on the way to a black-tie affair, with your lace thong pulled to the side and a gorgeous dress covering the rest of you."

Her eyes blaze with lust, and her breathing intensifies.

"And sometimes I'll want to grab your hair, gather it in my fist, and pull it hard. I'll say harsh, filthy words in your ear that make you wet and hot," I growl, and she runs her tongue over her teeth. "Every now and then, or maybe more, I'll want to smack that lush ass till it's red, then kiss it until it doesn't smart any longer. I want to pin your wrists over your head and fuck you hard and deep, and then even deeper till you beg me to let you come." The look on her face turns hazy, like she's coated in a fine dusting of lust. "But right now..." My voice turns softer as I trail off.

"Yes?" she asks, as if she can't bear to be left hanging, and it shows in her breasts—they're heaving, and it's fucking incredible. It's as if we exist in a cocoon of heat and color and shimmer. I have never wanted a woman the way I want her—deep in my bones.

I run my thumb across her jaw, and she leans into my touch. "Right now, I'm going to make love to you."

"Oh God," she says, her pitch rising. "Please. Now. I can't take it anymore. I want you so much."

She spears her fingers through my hair and crushes her lips to my mouth. Her tongue sweeps across mine and she moans. I swallow the sound—I swallow all her hungry noises as I undo her zipper, then peel her jeans down her hips.

We break the kiss so I can get these damn clothes off her. Her shirt flies to the ground in a flurry of clothes—hers, mine, both—pooling on the dark hardwood floor.

As I gaze on her naked figure, I am in awe.

It's not because her body is beautiful, though it is.

It's not because the curve of her hips, and the shape of her breasts, and the softness of her skin send my temperature to incendiary levels.

Though they do.

No. This astonishment is something that's harder to label, tougher to pin down. It's in the air; it's in the electricity. It's in the energy that draws her to me.

It's her.

It's just fucking her.

"Come," I say, scooping her up and setting her on the bed so her dark hair fans across the crisp white pillowcase. "Tonight I'm going to worship you. I'm going to adore you."

"You already do." She trembles as she lies naked in front of me. I'm floored, utterly floored that she's back in my life, and I want to give her everything.

I also happen to know exactly how she likes one little wonderful thing in particular.

And though she parts her legs for me, inviting me to pay a much-needed visit to that pretty pink pussy with my mouth, I wiggle an eyebrow and shake my head.

"Please stop torturing me. You know I love your mouth. I want you now."

"I know, my Penny. I know you want me," I say, my eyes cast down to those lovely plump lips, so fantastically wet they glisten. I climb over her, grab one hip, and flip her to her belly.

She gasps my name, in a long, lingering moan. *"Gabriel."*

As I grab a pillow and slide it under her stomach, I ease my body against her, my front to her back. "Did you think I'd forget what drives you wild?"

"Oh God," she says, her breath coming fast. Then I move down her body, and she's wriggling and arching up her hips, and Jesus Fucking Christ, she's inviting me to the promised land between her legs.

"Such a greedy woman." I spread my palms over the backs of her thighs, opening her more. She's so wet and slick, and I'm dying to taste her.

Raising her ass up higher, I bring my face to her beautiful pussy and I moan as I flick my tongue across her arousal.

"Oh my God," she calls out, arching up instantly.

Her taste floods my tongue. Her scent fills my nostrils, and all the blood in my body diverts to my cock. I'm so fucking hard as I lick her, as I taste her, as I lap up all this ridiculously wonderful wetness.

And Penny, she's a live wire. She's a writhing, hot, beautiful wave in my bed. My eyes drift to her hands. Fisted tightly, they clutch at my sheets, grasping. I glance down her legs, and her toes are curled, digging into my bed.

And here, right here in my mouth, she's the way I want her.

So fucking wet.

So fucking hot.

So fucking turned on.

She rocks her hips and her ass back into me, practically thrashing on the bed. My hands are wrapped around her thighs, and my tongue flicks over the delicious rise of her clit.

Her cries transform. Louder. Longer. Higher. A collection of *I'm so close*, and *yes*, and then just *oh, oh, oh, oh, oh*.

I devour her, kissing her lovely pussy until she shatters.

She unleashes the most glorious sound from her throat—a strangled and beautiful cry of rapture that might be my name, or God's name, or just an incoherent string of syllables to punctuate her pleasure as she detonates.

* * * *

Penny

At some point—maybe in a week, maybe a year—this orgasm might recede.

Might.

For now, I'm drunk. I'm high. I'm under the influence of some kind of euphoria.

This man.

This night.

Us.

As I blink open my eyes, he's flipped me back over again, and I can't think of anything but this exquisite ache between my legs, which was sated but has returned instantly. I need more of him. All of him.

He kneels over me, his hand wrapped around his cock, stroking.

God, he's gorgeous—his long hair, his ink-covered arms, his lean, toned abs. And his cock. I don't think I could even say that word in my head when I was twenty-one. All I knew then was I wanted it inside me. Now, I can't stop staring at his cock—long, thick, curved.

My mouth goes dry. I want him so much.

My skin is burning. This is a fever, and I don't want to bring my temperature down.

I want to take him into me. I want to be filled by him. Only him. Always him. It's only ever been him.

I reach for his shoulders, pulling him closer. I'm not sure I can speak again. When he rubs the head of his cock through all that wetness between my legs, my brain shuts down. I simply combust. It's as if I'm having an out-of-body experience within my body. It's as if I've become one with the physical, and everything in me is connected to him.

Somehow, the wires in my brain reattach enough for me to say what's in my heart. "*Please.* I need you. Please get inside me."

He slides his cock across me, teasing me more, driving me absolutely out of my mind. My hips arch off the bed, my nails dig into his flesh, and my chest heats to dangerous levels. Every molecule in my body is white-hot.

"*Penny.*" His voice has never been huskier with me, never been rougher.

"Yes?"

"Are you on the pill?"

I nod quickly. "Yes, God yes. Are you safe?"

"I am."

And that's all. He sinks into me, and I cry out.

I do. I just fucking do.

He fills me completely—so far and deep, and so fucking perfect. Lowering to his elbows, his chest to mine, his eyes on me, he's as close as he can be as he thrusts. As he strokes. As he rocks into me.

He groans my name as his cock stretches me, and the tip hits me so intensely that I scream out.

Not in pain, but in pleasure. Oh God, in so much pleasure I don't know how I can keep it all inside me. I feel as if I'm going to burst with ecstasy, that all of this intensity will spill over, and yet I crave more.

I have more than enough bliss. I have more than I need, but I'm greedy and I want it all with him.

His hands rope into my hair, and he fucks and he fucks and he fucks, his hips driving powerfully into me.

"God, it's good. It's so fucking good. It's you," he rasps.

"Yes. Yes. *Yes.*" It's all I can say. Because it's all I can feel. The answer to everything is yes.

I hook my legs tighter around his ass, my fingers curling through his hair, and I do everything to draw him in closer. Deeper.

Existence around us fades, burning away into nothingness, to pure darkness. Because all the starlight in my world is here with him. With this man I fell for ten years ago. Now, I'm not just falling.

I'm there.

I'm in love.

And it isn't just any kind. It's the big kind. The crazy kind. The type of love that latches on to you and won't let go. I bring my mouth to his ear, ready to tell him, ready to share my whole heart, but then he pushes so deep into me that I see stars. I see the light of distant planets. I see entire universes. It's that good. It's that intense.

I unravel in the most mind-bending, breathtaking, toe-curling kind of climax. It unfurls. It spreads, and the aftershocks roll through me as he chases me there, coming and not stopping. Just like me, just like him, just like us.

He's loud. Hot, and rough, and sexy.

I barely know what he's saying, because he's speaking another language, but it's carnal and dirty and so fucking beautiful.

The next words, though, I understand them perfectly.

He collapses onto my chest. "*Je t'aime*," he breathes into my neck.

And I soar. "I love you, Gabriel. I fell in love with you then. I'm in love with you now."

"The same, my love. It's completely the same for me."

* * * *

Gabriel

We eat.

We drink.

We devour dessert and each other.

Not necessarily in that order. Or any order. The whole night is one big fiesta of consumption—of food and wine and treats and her.

And after the third time, or perhaps the fourth, we're sweaty and slick, and her breasts are red, and she looks perfectly manhandled by me. A shower sounds nice, but when I wrap my arm around her, she yawns, and I decide that the morning is for washing up.

"Sleep with me," I whisper into her hair.

"Mmm," she murmurs. "I think I'm nearly there."

I kiss her shoulder lightly, dusting my lips across her flowers, and she runs her fingertips over the map on my arm as we drift off.

Before sleep covers us, though, I press one more kiss to her forehead. "Have I told you how happy I am that my restaurant was on your list for your event? If it wasn't, I don't know how we'd be here like this."

"Me, too."

"Do you know what I regret most about losing your email back then?"

She raises her face, her eyes less sleepy now. "No. Tell me."

"That I didn't get to tell you I was falling in love with you. So you'll have to forgive me if I can't stop saying it now."

The way she looks at me, her smile, her eyes, it's as if every moment in my life has led to this. "Say it."

I cup her cheeks in my hands. "I love you."

"Again," she demands playfully.

"I'm madly in love with you."

"Once more."

"I love you more than I knew was possible," I say, then I spoon against her and brush kisses along the back of her neck. "Sometimes it feels like the last ten years happened, but didn't happen. Like we went from then to now."

She laughs. "I wish."

"Or maybe it just feels like you've always been mine. That even though I didn't see you for a decade, you were mine." It's the caveman in me talking. But it's the man, too.

"I was yours," she says. "I am yours. And you're mine."

The past doesn't matter anymore.

Chapter Fourteen

Gabriel

Some kind of wiry terrier dog laps up water greedily from a bowl, while a rust-colored canine sniffs the grass. When the red dog finds something that, presumably, is tasty to her doggy senses, she opens her mouth to lunge for it.

"Ruby, no!"

From my spot by the tables, where my cooks and servers are ably handling the catering, I wave to Penny's friend Nicole.

Penny introduced me to Delaney and Nicole earlier this week. She wanted me to meet her friends, and we went out for drinks at Speakeasy in Midtown, savoring Purple Snow Globe cocktails. That turned into dinner, which unspooled into the women insisting I find the best ice cream in all of Manhattan for them.

I didn't mind. Penny's friends are wonderful, and they clearly love her fiercely. I took them to a small-batch shop in Murray Hill with bizarre flavor combinations like blueberry goat cheese, avocado graham cracker, and fire-roasted strawberry. The latter was Penny's favorite.

She liked it, too, when we said good-bye to her friends and returned to her home, where we discovered how very much she likes having her wrists tied to the headboard with a silk scarf.

Shortcake didn't, though.

Her little dog barked when she found her mistress trussed up. Good little dog, however, as soon as Penny told her to lie down in her dog bed, the tiny creature listened and I had my wicked way with

Penny.

Over and over and over.

Every night with her has been both a discovery and a rediscovery. When we collided in Spain, we were a meteor shower. The clock had ticked relentlessly then, and we were urgent, first-time lovers. Now, we're the night sky, together at the end of each day, and there's just as much urgency but also a deeper curiosity to try and test. The first time around, she was young and innocent but she was ready.

And last night, she said to me, "I want you to take my body. I want to explore everything with you."

Yeah.

I didn't need to be asked twice. It's like winning the lottery— finding this wonderful woman who wants me the same way I do her, then finding her again. Being her first. Being the one she wants now.

And now, as I stand under the warm afternoon sun in Central Park, I'm uncomfortably aroused in the presence of all these dogs, volunteers, shelter donors, and men and women who've just finished running the 5K.

Including Penny, who's here with Shortcake. Penny chats with a blond guy in glasses, who has a huge mastiff by his side. When she spots me, her eyes light up and she waves. I make my way to her to say hello, and I extend a hand to the guy.

"Mitch, this is Gabriel Mathias," she says. "He owns Gabriel's on Christopher and has been gracious enough to cater the event. You have to try one of the mini sandwiches. You'll love it."

Mitch rubs his belly. "Can't wait."

Penny turns to me. "And Gabriel, this is Mitch and his dog, Charlie. Mitch is one of my dog park friends."

We chat about the weather and the city for a minute, until Mitch and the big beast head to the food.

Penny leans in closer and whispers, "We went out twice."

I straighten as an unexpected dose of jealousy rushes through me. "You did?"

She smiles softly. "Yes, but it was nothing. He's very sweet, but we had no spark." She stands on tiptoe and brushes her lips across my neck. "Not like with you. It's all spark."

A low rumble works its way up my chest, but the jealousy isn't replaced by the lust. Not yet. "Two dates, you say? You must have liked him enough to go on two dates."

She rolls her eyes. "Settle down. Like I said, we didn't connect." She places her palm on my chest. "I just wanted to tell you. To be open. Okay?"

Her eyes pin me with a searing, honest look that tells me this is part of how we navigate the new terrain. "Yes, of course," I say, and then I cup the back of her head, threading my hand in her hair, and I kiss her possessively.

Perhaps more possessively than usual.

I might even dip her, bring her chest to mine, and rope an arm around her back as my lips claim hers. Quite possibly I consider biting her. I find the will to resist somehow.

When we break the kiss, she blinks then brushes her hand down her shirt. "Are you marking me?"

With narrowed eyes, I nod. "Perhaps I am."

She laughs, curls her dog's leash tighter around her hand, then says, "Duly noted. And now it's time for me to chat with donors."

"Go," I say, encouragingly. I return to the food tents, chat with the servers and the cooks, and jump in from time to time to help serve. I say hello to the attendees, make conversation, and do everything possible to ensure the event is a huge success.

By all accounts it is, judging from the sheer number of people, and dogs, and happy faces. Penny is in the midst of it with her little butterscotch dog, who is quite the ambassador for the shelter. They both mingle with the attendees and a burst of pride suffuses me.

This is her element. Her love. Her passion. I'm lucky enough to watch her in action and witness the impact she has on other dog lovers. I couldn't be happier to have my restaurant connected with her event, and as the festivities start to wind down, I make my way out of the tent and across the lawn, chatting with some of my business associates on the way.

I stop when I see a tall and broad man make his way to Penny. He's out of place, wearing slacks, and a button-down when nearly everyone is casual. His hair is cropped short, military-style almost. And I hate instantly that women flock to him. His lopsided grin and the way a handful of ladies check him out tell me he isn't hurting in that department.

When he makes a beeline for Penny, I tilt my head, studying them.

I can't make out their conversation from this many feet away. I remind myself it's not my place to interfere, and I keep moving through the crowds, spotting a familiar burnished dog and the redhead with her.

Ah, Nicole.

She leans close to Delaney, and they have that protective shoulder-to-shoulder stance women take when they look out for their own. Delaney's fists are clenched, and as I walk behind them, their words are like a jolt of electricity.

"I'm so glad she didn't marry that ass," Delaney hisses to Nicole.

"*So* glad she didn't marry Captain Asshole," Nicole seconds.

Let me revise that.

More like an electric shock.

Chapter Fifteen

Penny

With his fancy duds, Gavin is out of place. But the man always loved looking the part of the player. Of the smooth, suave New York man-about-town.

Or the sky, really.

When we were together, he played up the whole sexy pilot angle every chance he had. And it worked on me for a while.

Now, he does nothing for me. But he's one of our regular donors, and despite his inability to keep his dick in his pants, he's done a lot to help the dogs, and all of our biggest supporters were invited to attend today.

Funny how you might want to despise someone but can't, since he isn't all bad. Gavin was a regular thousand-dollar-a-month donor before we dated, and he has continued to give freely after we split. His job makes it impossible for him to have pets, so he has chosen to give to my shelter instead.

"How's everything going in the friendly skies?" I ask, trying to keep it light as I shield my eyes.

"Totally great," he says in a smooth, confident tone as he takes off his aviator shades and hooks them on the neck of his button-down. "I picked up a new international route to Paris, and one to Vienna. I've been trying to take advantage of all the great culture in those cities."

I bet he has. "You can't beat Europe for culture. What's been your favorite thing so far?" I ask, keeping up the small talk.

"I'd have to say Paris," he says, and as he talks my mind drifts to Gabriel, and to how much I want to explore the world with him. He has such an adventuresome spirit, and it pairs perfectly with my own.

"But I have to say, being there reminded me of one thing."

"What's that?" I ask nicely, trying to stay engaged.

Gavin steps closer, inches away from me. At my feet, Shortcake lets out a low growl. We're away from the crowd, standing near an oak tree on a grassy knoll.

"It's okay, girl," I say to my dog, then look up at Gavin again. He's still as handsome as ever with his green eyes, square jaw, and broad shoulders. But he's only empirically attractive. He might have a heart for animals, but he hasn't yet learned how to treat women.

"What's on my mind is why you didn't answer my email. That's why I came here today."

Oh no. I dig my heels into the ground and square my shoulders. I don't want to get into something with him. "Gavin, I didn't answer your email because it's over with us."

He nods like he understands, but then clasps his hands together in a plea. "But what about a second chance? Do you believe in second chances?"

I scrunch my forehead as if he's crazy. I believe in them so much he'd be shocked. But not between us, and I'm surprised he has the audacity to show up with that line. "In this case, no. I don't believe in second chances. Not after the way we ended," I say, keeping my tone even. Truthfully, if we weren't here in public, I'd have some choice words for him. I'd let him know precisely where he could stick his wandering one-eyed monster. But he's not worth putting the event at risk. "Gavin, I appreciate all you do for the shelter, but I hope you can understand that it's over with us."

He reaches for my arm. I step back. He moves closer. "Penny," he pleads. "I know you always wanted to get married. Let's just put the past behind us and tie the knot. You and me and Shortcake," he says, with a little quirk of his lips like he thinks using my dog's name will get me to say yes.

Shortcake lifts an ear when she hears her name.

I open my mouth to speak.

But someone else gets a word in first.

"She said no."

I nearly stumble with relief to find Gabriel by my side.

Gavin's eyes widen, then narrow. "I believe this is between Penny and me."

Gabriel holds up one finger and says in a cool, sophisticated tone, "Ah, but that's where you're wrong. It's not between the two of you, since she's with me now." He ropes an arm around my shoulders and grips me hard.

Gavin's green eyes flick from me to Gabriel then back.

"Besides," Gabriel continues, "I believe she told you no, not after the way it ended. Perhaps you'd like to take that as your cue to run along."

And in case there was any doubt, Gabriel cups my cheek with his other hand and delivers a crushing kiss to my mouth. He's definitely marking me now, and I can feel it in the way his teeth graze over my lips. This kiss feels like a punishment as much as a claiming.

After five seconds, he pulls away and flashes a practiced smile at my ex. "But thank you for being a supporter of Little Friends and the dogs. Be sure to have a sandwich on the way out."

Gavin rubs his knuckle against his ear, like he can't quite believe that another man has bested him. He raises his hand in a faint wave and wanders off, a scolded child searching aimlessly for a new toy.

Gabriel turns to me, cocks his head, and speaks ever-so-softly, but in the crispest voice. "Now, love. Is there anyone else I should expect to run into today at this event?"

And whatever anger radiates off him—I seize it and hold it for myself. "What the hell? Why would you say that?" I whisper-yell at him.

He lifts his chin. "Let's see. I've already bumped into someone you dated, and now, apparently, that asshole you were nearly married to." He strokes his chin. "Funny, you never mentioned him."

The anger doubles down. It triples. How dare he? "You didn't want to hear! And I was never almost married to Gavin. And I should *not* have to apologize for having gone on two dates with Mitch, who is, incidentally, a very nice guy," I say through thin lips, as I point in the general direction of the crowd.

"But what about Captain Asshole? The one trying to win you back?"

Out of the corner of my eye I spot Lacey walking toward with me with another one of our biggest donors.

I breathe in through my nose, willing my heart to settle and my frustration to take a hike. I lower my voice more and say to Gabriel, "I can't talk about this now. I need to chat with one of our donors." He arches an eyebrow at that last word, as if he's caught me being a...a playgirl? "And you're being entirely unfair."

He drops a gentle kiss to my cheek, but his words aren't sweet. "What's entirely unfair is that you were so focused on my past, and it bothered you immensely, and that was all because of what you *heard* the press say about me. Now in the span of a few hours, I've come face-to-face with two of your exes." He puts his hand on his chest. "Call me crazy, but that's not exactly my favorite thing to experience. And that's why, perhaps, it's best that I not be in this vicinity right now." He takes a breath. "I just need to be by myself for a bit."

He leaves, and that frustration inside me explodes into hurt and sadness as I watch him walk away, because it brings back all the bitter memories of the evening at the fountain.

But there's no time to talk. I have to slip on a happy face. Shortcake wags her tail, like she knows only a dog's love will do right now. I bend down, scratch her chin, then plaster on a smile and focus on business while my heart aches cruelly.

Chapter Sixteen

Gabriel

Fifth Avenue is a zoo.

I lower my sunglasses over my eyes and push through the throngs of Saturday-afternoon New Yorkers—hipsters in cuffed jeans and horn-rimmed glasses, mothers in capri pants pushing sporty strollers next to fathers in striped shirts, young couples with their hands in each other's back pockets, wearing flirty smiles that hint of afternoon delights to come.

I'm not in the fucking mood for crowds, or people, or being civilized, and if I'd stayed at that event a second longer, I'd have said something I'd really regret. With my fists clenched and red clouds billowing from my ears, I'd walked away from the picnic and across the park to Fifth Avenue, and now I'm heading south, right next to a goddamn bus that somehow keeps the same pace as I do.

Acrid fumes blow from the giant vehicle's exhaust. I drag a hand roughly through my hair. Frustration digs deep inside me, tunneling through my body, setting up camp in my bones.

Because...Penny.

Fucking Penny.

And Mitch and Gavin.

As the bus rumbles to a stop, I can't deal with this sardine-feel of New York.

I cross the avenue, heading east along a side street in the sixties, doing my best to get away from the heart of the city. Away from the woman in the park who brings out this side of me that I don't like.

Grabbing my phone, I click on the playlist I made last week thanks to Tina's recommendations. But Pizza for Breakfast reminds me of Penny, so I find a classical piece—a cello number Tina used to play, she told me. Popping in my earbuds, I crank the music up and turn off all the other apps on my phone. Not that Penny has called. Not that Penny has texted. Not that she wants to talk to me, either.

Maybe it's for the best. I don't know what I'd say now.

I'm not sure why I feel...deceived? Enraged? Hurt?

But I don't know that those fit entirely.

Pissed?

That works. She should have told me she'd almost married someone, shouldn't she? She should have damn well let me know. I don't want to run into her ex-boyfriend at the park. Or anywhere.

Especially considering she was bothered by the things that had been said about me.

That's what's gnawing at me.

But as the soothing notes of the cello bathe my brain, and New York starts to feel less like a carnival, I know that's not it, either.

I wander past a bookstore. A book on modern art sits in the window, a new coffee-table hardback with full-color photos and a Mark Rothko on the cover. It catches my eye, and I stop and stare. The image reminds me of the night we went to the Museum of Modern Art.

The thoughts start to untangle from the ball of anger inside me. All the fuzzy ideas in my head sharpen.

It's not her. It's me.

As I recall our conversation in front of the Pollock at MoMa, Tina's words to me about identity, and my own words to Penny, rise up in front of me.

It's not my identity as the *playboy chef* that I'll have a hard time giving up, like Tina had suggested. That's not an issue at all. Sure, I've had a past. Yes, I've enjoyed the company of women. But giving up an amorous lifestyle for one woman who rocks my world? Ha. That's the easiest thing to do. I don't miss the merry-go-round. Penny is all I'll ever need or want.

But Tina wasn't wrong when she mentioned identity. Only, the issue isn't how I see myself, but how I picture Penny.

And I said as much at the museum the other night.

"Besides, my brain has played this fantastic trick on me. It blots out any thought of what you've been doing from the moment you left Barcelona until you walked into my restaurant the other day."

Penny is the sweet, innocent girl I met in Barcelona, and she's the sexy, confident woman I know today. She's the virgin and the lover. She's the woman she was then, and the woman she is now.

But she's also been herself for ten years, too, and I've blotted that out.

I've erased those ten years of her life without me.

I've only ever seen her as mine. And I may only want her to be mine, but to see her that way is terribly unfair to the woman she is today—the woman I've fallen in love with anew. That's what set me off. Not whether she told me about some ass she dated—we've all gone out with jerks—but that my illusion of her as mine and only ever mine has been shattered.

And that's okay.

To keep moving forward, I have to accept that she's had a whole life in between Barcelona and two weeks ago.

Maybe I don't need details. I certainly don't want to linger on those thoughts, especially since I'm sure she doesn't have a long trail of men behind her. But at the very least, I can't let a normal, reasonable dating history get the better of me. And I can't let it ruin this chance to be with the one I love.

She's not pure as the driven snow like she joked. She's not supposed to be. Neither am I.

We just need to only have eyes for each other now, and I know we do, and we will.

I also need to say I am sorry for being a jealous ass. She brings out that side of me, but only because I want her all to myself, all the time.

As I step away from the bookstore, I look at the time and pick up the pace, my long stride eating up the sidewalk as I return to the park.

I stop in my tracks, though, when I pass a candy store.

Chapter Seventeen

Penny

I make it through to the end of the event. I talk to donors. I play with dogs. I scratch the chins of Labs, and stroke the backs of dachshunds, and shake the paws of Jack Russell terriers.

The event is a smash hit, and it looks as if we're ahead of our fundraising goals. Also, everyone's been raving about the food and buzzing about wanting to visit Gabriel's restaurant.

Me?

I haven't touched a thing.

As I finish my last few conversations and then wrap up with Lacey, I try once more to will away the pang in my chest.

Drawing a deep breath, I remind myself that I've gotten over hurt before. I've moved past the particular kind of pain that love inflicts. I can handle this wound.

But as I say good-bye to my assistant, that twinge resurfaces. It's a new, fresh cut, different from the one inflicted ten years ago when he didn't show at the fountain. Because this one comes after the most wonderful reunion I could ever have dreamed up.

A little whimper sounds from beside my feet. I glance at Shortcake, who has conked out on the grass. Tired from her role as a mascot for the shelter, she lounges on the cool, green blanket of the ground.

"I like the way you think." I flop next to her. She takes that as an offer to lick my face. As she sweeps her tongue across my cheek, I laugh.

And the laughter feels good.

It reminds me that life is good, and love is good, and that maybe I shouldn't be quick to close the door. Just because I've been hurt before doesn't mean it'll happen again. Just because we fought doesn't mean we're through. Love isn't all or nothing. It's a million variations, and some days are better than others. Some are luminous, and others are muted, but none of them mean the end. I'd assumed Gabriel's absence for the last two hours meant we'd reached the finish line. But maybe it just means he needed to cool off.

Like Shortcake is doing.

I tug her close and kiss her sweet little butterscotch face. "I love you," I tell her, and she responds with a speed-round of kisses.

"She has the right idea."

I sit bolt upright when I hear his voice.

"Hi," I say, and I push my hands on the ground to stand. But he's faster, and he parks himself next to me. He holds a small white paper bag, the top folded over.

"I'm sorry," he says, contrition in his voice and etched deep in his eyes.

"I'm glad, because you really were being unfair," I say, my voice soft—but strong, too, as I speak my piece. "You didn't want to know about the past. You said as much."

His smile is rueful. "I know, love. I know. Because I want you all to myself, and that's not fair."

"But you have me, Gabriel. Don't you know that?"

"I do." His eyes plead with me. "Forgive me."

"Of course." My lips twitch. "And I'm sorry, too."

He tilts his head. "What are you sorry for? I was the asshole."

Laughing lightly, I say, "Because I never mentioned Gavin."

He shakes his head and places a hand on my arm. Shortcake scoots between us and licks his forearm, working on the map of Europe. He strokes her head, and damn if that sight doesn't just slay me. "No, my love. You're not required to give me your dating résumé. It was ridiculous for me to react that way—like a jealous ass."

My lips curve into a grin. "Weirdly, I like your jealous side. Well, some of it," I amend.

He laughs. "Which part?"

I angle my body closer to his. "The part that makes you want me all to yourself."

"But that's all of me," he says, as my dog raises her snout and sniffs the white bag. "And that's why I want to apologize. I reacted badly because I think of you as all mine. Since I was your first." As he says it, everything makes sense. His comments. His reactions. His possessiveness.

"You feel an ownership of me?"

He nods. "I suppose I do. But that's not fair. I know ten years passed, and of course you've had other relationships. It's foolish of me to think you've only ever been with me, even if that's what the jealous fool in me wants. But it's not fair for me to expect you to have detailed every relationship for me. Especially since I pretty much told you at the museum that I preferred to think of you as having no history." His grin is wry and his tone self-deprecating.

I reach for his hair, playing with the ends. "I've dated some over the years, but mostly I've been focused on dogs, and work, and my friends. I'm not someone who sleeps around. And you also need to know, I was never engaged to Gavin. I thought that he might propose, but he didn't, and if he had, I'd have said no. I left him because he was a cheater. He had affairs left and right."

Gabriel sneers. "Ass. He's unworthy of any woman."

"But that's not the biggest reason why it ended."

His brow furrows. "Why did it end?"

I tiptoe my fingers up his hair. I love his long hair—the lush, soft strands, the sexy, rock-star look of him. "I didn't love him deeply. I didn't love him at all, actually."

"No?"

I shake my head and lower my voice. "My heart was given a long time ago, in Park Güell. No one else has ever come close," I say, and this is the true vulnerability. This is my heart on the line.

He presses his forehead to mine and sighs deeply, happily. Then he whispers, "It's only ever been you, Penny." He pulls back, runs the pads of his fingers across my chin, and meets my gaze. "You're the only one for me."

I lean in to kiss him but he holds up a finger. "I bought you a little something."

"You did?"

"When a man messes up, he should always bring a woman a gift. He should say he's sorry, he should give her a gift, and there's one more thing he should do. But first...this." He opens the small, white, paper bag, reaches in, and takes out an even smaller bag.

Of caramels.

"Your favorite candy. You told me so the day we met. It has always reminded me of you."

I beam. It's just candy, but that's the point. It's candy because he's sorry, and because he's with me, and because that's what you do when you've hurt the one you love. Then you move on. You keep going. You put it behind you.

"Take a bite," he says, reaching for a wrapped candy from the bag. "I like the way you taste with caramel on your tongue." He strokes his chin. "Scratch that. I always like the way you taste."

He curls his hand around mine and kisses me deeply. It tastes like the past, like the present, and like all our tomorrows.

But I'm wildly curious about something he left unanswered, so I break the kiss and tap his shoulder. "What's the third thing a man should do when he's messed up?"

He rises, reaches for my hand, and pulls me up. "Why don't we go back to your place, and I'll show you."

And that night at my home, that's when he gives me more orgasms than I can count.

All things considered, I think I came out okay from this little tiff in the park. As the night blurs to an end, and the early light of the dawn peeks through the blinds, we fall asleep at last—him, me, and Shortcake, who's wedged herself between us.

Epilogue

Gabriel

Two months later

The clock tells me it's nearly six in the evening. We have plans for dinner and to see a show. I've been here for ten minutes, since I arrived early.

The fountains beat out a watery rhythm behind me. A chill seeps through the air as the shorter days and longer nights bear down on New York City.

I wait for her. Briefly, I flash back to how she must have felt waiting and think how hard it must have been for her.

I know how hard it was for me to be on the other side of the world.

When I spot her walking up the steps, I stop rewinding to the past. Tonight, we write a new story.

My gorgeous Penny wears a short, black jacket, cinched at the waist. And heels, always heels. And does she ever look stunning with her lovely legs on display. Her hair falls long and loose, and my mind forms a fantastic image of curling those strands around my fist later.

But now is not the time for such thoughts.

As she nears me, she grins. I cross the final distance to her and take her in my arms. I say nothing—I simply kiss her. I can't resist. She melts against me, and that's what I want. Always and forever.

When we separate, she gives me a breathy hello.

"Good evening to you," I say as my hand travels up the front of her jacket to her collar, where a splash of red fabric shows. "Red dress?"

She shrugs sexily. "Seemed fitting since you asked me to meet you here," she says, tipping her head toward the fountain.

I take a breath. "I wanted us to have a chance to do this part over, too. The fountain part. To have what we didn't have here the first time," I say, my eyes locked with hers. Her lips part slightly. "Now that we're together again, I believe it was meant to be this way, and we were meant to meet a second time. I believe if we'd been here ten years ago, we'd have messed up our chances somehow. Made mistakes. Been too young and foolish."

A smile spreads across her face. "Maybe we'd each have done things to push the other away. Maybe we'd have lost each other."

My heart lifts, knowing she understands me. She gets me. "What if we needed those years apart so we could get it right the second time around?"

Her eyes shine with happiness, and I'm sure mine do, too. "I think we're getting it right. Don't you?"

Taking her hands in mine, I drop to one knee. Her eyes widen, and she whispers my name. It sounds heavenly on her lips and I'm hopeful—so damn hopeful—she wants this as much as I do. I take the ring from my pocket and hold up a brilliant, emerald-cut diamond.

"Let's get it right for always. Forever. Will you marry me?"

Tears fall from her eyes, and she drops to her knees, too, wrapping her arms around me. "Yes, yes, yes."

Penny

Sometimes heartbreak happens for a reason. Sometimes hurt does make us stronger. At the time, I couldn't have imagined that this place—the most romantic spot in all of Manhattan—could be anything but the epicenter of all my regret. Now, as a gem sparkles brightly on my finger and the lights twinkle around us while the fountains spray merrily in the twilight sky, we start a brand new tale. A happily ever after that unfolds in front of us.

"I always hoped somehow I'd see you again," I tell him through my tears.

"My love, you're going to do more than see me. You'll see me every day now."

"That sounds like fate to me."

Yes, some things were meant to be.

THE END

Sign up for the 1001 Dark Nights Newsletter
and be entered to win a Tiffany Key necklace.

There's a contest every month!

Go to www.1001DarkNights.com to subscribe.

As a bonus, all subscribers will receive a free
1001 Dark Nights story
The First Night
by Lexi Blake & M.J. Rose

Turn the page for a full list of the
1001 Dark Nights fabulous novellas...

Discover 1001 Dark Nights Collection Three

HIDDEN INK by Carrie Ann Ryan
A Montgomery Ink Novella

BLOOD ON THE BAYOU by Heather Graham
A Cafferty & Quinn Novella

SEARCHING FOR MINE by Jennifer Probst
A Searching For Novella

DANCE OF DESIRE by Christopher Rice

ROUGH RHYTHM by Tessa Bailey
A Made In Jersey Novella

DEVOTED by Lexi Blake
A Masters and Mercenaries Novella

Z by Larissa Ione
A Demonica Underworld Novella

FALLING UNDER YOU by Laurelin Paige
A Fixed Trilogy Novella

EASY FOR KEEPS by Kristen Proby
A Boudreaux Novella

UNCHAINED by Elisabeth Naughton
An Eternal Guardians Novella

HARD TO SERVE by Laura Kaye
A Hard Ink Novella

DRAGON FEVER by Donna Grant
A Dark Kings Novella

KAYDEN/SIMON by Alexandra Ivy/Laura Wright
A Bayou Heat Novella

STRUNG UP by Lorelei James
A Blacktop Cowboys® Novella

MIDNIGHT UNTAMED by Lara Adrian
A Midnight Breed Novella

TRICKED by Rebecca Zanetti
A Dark Protectors Novella

DIRTY WICKED by Shayla Black
A Wicked Lovers Novella

THE ONLY ONE by Lauren Blakely
A One Love Novella

SWEET SURRENDER by Liliana Hart
A MacKenzie Family Novella

Go to www.1001DarkNights.com for more information.

Discover 1001 Dark Nights Collection One

FOREVER WICKED by Shayla Black
CRIMSON TWILIGHT by Heather Graham
CAPTURED IN SURRENDER by Liliana Hart
SILENT BITE: A SCANGUARDS WEDDING by Tina Folsom
DUNGEON GAMES by Lexi Blake
AZAGOTH by Larissa Ione
NEED YOU NOW by Lisa Renee Jones
SHOW ME, BABY by Cherise Sinclair
ROPED IN by Lorelei James
TEMPTED BY MIDNIGHT by Lara Adrian
THE FLAME by Christopher Rice
CARESS OF DARKNESS by Julie Kenner

Also from 1001 Dark Nights

TAME ME by J. Kenner

Go to www.1001DarkNights.com for more information.

Discover 1001 Dark Nights Collection Two

WICKED WOLF by Carrie Ann Ryan
WHEN IRISH EYES ARE HAUNTING by Heather Graham
EASY WITH YOU by Kristen Proby
MASTER OF FREEDOM by Cherise Sinclair
CARESS OF PLEASURE by Julie Kenner
ADORED by Lexi Blake
HADES by Larissa Ione
RAVAGED by Elisabeth Naughton
DREAM OF YOU by Jennifer L. Armentrout
STRIPPED DOWN by Lorelei James
RAGE/KILLIAN by Alexandra Ivy/Laura Wright
DRAGON KING by Donna Grant
PURE WICKED by Shayla Black
HARD AS STEEL by Laura Kaye
STROKE OF MIDNIGHT by Lara Adrian
ALL HALLOWS EVE by Heather Graham
KISS THE FLAME by Christopher Rice
DARING HER LOVE by Melissa Foster
TEASED by Rebecca Zanetti
THE PROMISE OF SURRENDER by Liliana Hart

Also from 1001 Dark Nights

THE SURRENDER GATE By Christopher Rice
SERVICING THE TARGET By Cherise Sinclair

Go to www.1001DarkNights.com for more information.

About Lauren Blakely

Since self-publishing her debut romance novel CAUGHT UP IN US over three years ago, Lauren Blakely has sold more than 1.5 million books. She is known for her sexy contemporary romance style that's full of heat, heart and humor. A devout fan of cake and canines, Lauren has plotted entire novels while walking her four-legged friends.

She lives in California with her family. With twelve New York Times bestsellers, her titles have appeared on the New York Times, USA Today, and Wall Street Journal Bestseller Lists more than seventy times. Her bestselling series include Sinful Nights, Seductive Nights, No Regrets, Caught Up in Love, and Fighting Fire as well as standalone hit romances like BIG ROCK, MISTER O, WELL HUNG, and THE SEXY ONE which were all instant New York Times Bestsellers.

In January she'll release FULL PACKAGE, a standalone romantic comedy. To receive an email when Lauren releases a new book, sign up for her newsletter here!

Full Package
By Lauren Blakely
Coming January 2017

I've been told I have quite a gift.

Hey, I don't just mean in my pants. I've got a big brain too, and a huge heart of gold. And I like to use all my gifts to the fullest, the package included. With the crazy stuff I deal with all day long at work, the one thing I want at night is to give a woman the time of her life, both in and out of bed.

But then I find myself stuck between a rock and a sexy roommate, which makes for one very hard…place.

Because scoring an apartment in this city is harder than finding true love. So even if I have to shack up with my buddy's smoking hot and incredibly amazing little sister, a man's got to do what a man's got to do.

I can resist Josie. I'm disciplined, I'm focused, and I keep my hands to myself, even in the mere five-hundred square feet we share. Until the one night she insists on sliding under the covers with me. It'll help her sleep after what happened that day, she says.

Surprise—neither one of us sleeps.

And even though we agree to return to roomies-without-benefits, I quickly realize I want more than someone to split the utilities with. Now all I want is to spend every night—and every day—with my gorgeous roommate.

Did I mention she's also one of my best friends? That she's brilliant, beautiful and a total firecracker? Guess that makes her the full package too.

What's a man stuck in a hard place to do?

Read on for chapter one from FULL PACKAGE, a standalone romantic comedy from Lauren Blakely, available in January 2017!

Chapter One

I have a theory that it takes the human brain at least three tries to fully process something when it's the opposite of what you want to hear.

Take now.

I'm on the third attempt.

Even though I can clearly hear the words the woman on the phone says, I'm sure if I repeat them in the form of a question, she'll eventually say what I want her to say. "I lost the apartment?" I try again, because soon the bad news she's serving up will magically morph into something good. Like if a rice cake turned into pizza. Preferably a cheese pie with mushrooms.

Because there is no fucking way the leasing agent is telling me *this*.

"The landlord had a change of heart," she says once more, and the sweet one-bedroom in Chelsea slips through my fingers.

I grit my teeth and suck in a breath as I pace outside the emergency room entrance at the hospital. The sidewalk is clogged with other doctors, too, as well as nurses and paramedics, not to mention visitors. I move away from them, walking along the brick exterior during this short break in my day. "But this is the fifth time a place has fallen through," I say, doing my best to keep my tone even. I don't have a temper. I don't get angry. But if I were to, this might be the reason. Because Dante was wrong. Finding an apartment in New York City is the tenth circle of hell. It's the eleventh, twelfth, and thirteenth, too.

Consider my luck so far in this impossible quest: the first apartment went bust when the landlord changed her mind. The second time, the place was rented to someone in the family. The third pad had termites. You get my drift.

"It's a tough market right now," Erica, the leasing agent, says. I gotta give her credit. She's been trying to find me four walls and a floor for more than a month. "I'll look again to see if there are any new available options."

"Thanks. My sublease is up so I'm going to be homeless soon." I turn around and pace back toward the entrance. Buying a place isn't an option. I've still got medical school debt, and doctors don't make bank the way they used to. Especially, not first-year ER docs.

She laughs. "I doubt you'll be homeless. Besides, I've told you, the couch at my place has your name on it. Come to think of it, so does the bed, if you know what I mean."

I blink. I do know what she means. I just wasn't expecting to be propositioned by my leasing agent at two in the afternoon on a Wednesday.

Or a Thursday. Or a Friday. Basically, on any day.

"Thanks for the offer." I rein in my surprise because I thought she was married. And not just the regular kind of married, but the happily kind.

"You let me know, Chase. I make a great ceviche, I'm incredibly neat, and I wouldn't even charge you a dime. We could work out some other form of payment," she says with a purr.

And my leasing agent has now officially requested that I be her boy toy. Fuck. Time to grow a beard. I know I look young for my job, but young enough to be asked to be a sugar-boy? I turn to the glass window of the hospital and consider my face. Clean-shaven, hazel eyes, light brown hair, chiseled jaw . . . Damn, I'm quite a specimen. No wonder she propositioned me. Maybe I should take her more seriously.

Even though I have zero interest in serving as anyone's sex slave, her offer is borderline tempting because I'm at the end of the line. I've scoured Craigslist and everyplace else, but I might as well give a kidney for a one-bedroom—that'd be easier than finding a pad in this city.

You know all those TV shows where the perky twenty-something advertising assistant nabs a swell apartment with a flower planter, bright purple walls, and a reading nook on the Upper West Side? Or when the wet-behind-the-ears dude with an entry-level post at a magazine lands a swank bachelor pad in Tribeca?

They lie.

At this point, I'd give my spleen just for a closet under a staircase. Wait, I take that back. I like my spleen. It'd have to be a closet on the first floor for me to give up an organ, even one I can easily live without.

"What do you think? You up for it?" Erica asks, in what no doubt is her best sexy-as-sin voice. "Bob said he's fine with you being here, too."

I frown. "Bob?" Immediately, I want to take back the question because I've got a sinking feeling Bob could be her vibrator, and I walked right into that one.

"Bob, my husband," she says matter-of-factly, and now I wish we were talking about a toy.

"That's quite generous of him," I deadpan. "And please let him know that while I appreciate his magnanimity, a mattress in the locker room just opened up."

I turn off my phone and head inside, my quick break over. Sandy, the curly-haired charge nurse, marches up to me, a serious look on her face as she tips her head toward the nearby exam room. But the tiniest twinkle in her gray eyes tells me my newest patient's situation isn't dire.

"Room two. Foreign body stuck in the forehead," she tells me. That's my cue to forget about square footage and unconventional living arrangements.

When I stride into the exam room, I find an angular, blond Aquaman perched on the edge of the hospital bed.

"I'm Doctor Summers. Nice threads." I flash a quick smile. Always helps to defuse the situation. And besides, if I reacted to the three-inch shard of glass sticking out of the forehead of the guy in the green costume, they should take my goddamn license away.

He shoots me a rueful grin as he glances at his getup. The polyester outfit is torn down the right arm and ripped along the thigh.

"Looks like a fun morning," I say, eyeing the crystal fragment in his skin. "Let me guess. Your forehead got intimately acquainted with a chandelier?"

He nods guiltily, the look in his eyes telling me he wasn't trying to fly.

"And let me hazard another guess." I stroke my chin. "You were trying to spice up your sex life by testing the whole idea of hanging from the chandeliers."

He swallows, gives another small nod, then an unsteady *yup*. "Can you get it out?"

"That's what she said," I say, and he chuckles. I pat his shoulder. "Couldn't resist, but the answer is yes, and there will only be a small scar. I'm excellent at stitches."

He takes a deep breath, and I get to work, numbing his forehead before I remove the glass. We chat as I go, making small talk about his fondness for superheroes, then I tell him the latest of my apartment hunt woes.

"Manhattan is crazy," he says. "Even in commercial real estate, it's all gone through the roof." Then he adds, almost sheepishly. "Though, I can't complain since that's my business."

"Smart man. Square footage in this city is like a precious jewel," I say as I finish work on the stitches.

Twenty minutes later, I've sewn up his forehead, and a nurse returns with the shard in a plastic Bio-hazard bag. She hands it to me, and I pass it on to the rightful owner.

"A souvenir of today's visit to the ER," I tell the guy, and he takes the bag.

"Thanks, Doc. The sad thing is we didn't even get to the main event."

"That's why it's an urban myth. You can't really do it while hanging from the chandelier. And hey, next time you're feeling adventurous, take a cooking class and then go home and use the table for dessert, okay? But make sure it's a nice, smooth wood because I don't want to have to remove a three-inch splinter from your gluteus maximus. That's not as good a war story."

He nods crisply. "I promise. No more acrobatics."

"But kudos on having a woman who likes you that much," I say as we leave the room.

He tilts his head. "How'd you know she likes me?"

I nod toward the row of chairs in the waiting room at the end of the hallway. A dark-haired woman in a busty emerald-green costume nibbles on her lip and checks her watch. When she raises her face, her eyes light up as they land on Aquaman.

"I'm guessing the mermaid brought you in? And waited for you?"

"Yeah," Aquaman says with a dopey smile as he looks at his woman.

"Bed tonight. Use the bed, man," I say in a low voice.

He gives me a thumbs up as he leaves.

And, that's today's latest chapter in the tales of the naughty deeds that land you in the ER. Yesterday, it was a zipper malfunction. Last week, it was a fracture from a back handspring. Yeah, you don't want to know what was fractured.

* * * *

Later, when my shift ends, I change into my street clothes in the locker room, button my jeans, and tug on a T-shirt. I rake my fingers through my hair, grab my shades, and leave the workday behind me. The second the doors slide shut at Mercy Hospital, I turn off the medical portion of my brain, plug in my headphones, and crank up the audiobook I've been listening to lately. It's on the theory of chaos, and it keeps me company as I head to Greenwich Village to meet a friend.

Once downtown, I leave the subway in a throng of New Yorkers on a warm June day and make my way to the Sugar Love Sweet Shop to meet my friend Josie.

Yes, this friend happens to possess boobs.

Because I have another theory—men and women can be friends. Great friends. Even if the woman happens to be the owner of the most fantastic pair of breasts this man has ever seen. A body is a body is a body. I can appreciate her figure empirically, in all its curves and softness, and that doesn't mean I want to hang from the chandeliers with her, or even screw her on a table.

Fine, I'll concede she's totally table screwable, but I don't let myself think of Josie that way.

Even if she looks amazing in that pink scoop-neck T-shirt and a cute little polka-dot apron tied around her waist.

When she spots me, she waves and calls me into the candy shop.

I go, and my mouth is only watering because I like sweet things.

On behalf of 1001 Dark Nights,

Liz Berry and M.J. Rose would like to thank ~

Steve Berry
Doug Scofield
Kim Guidroz
Jillian Stein
InkSlinger PR
Dan Slater
Asha Hossain
Chris Graham
Pamela Jamison
Fedora Chen
Jessica Johns
Dylan Stockton
Richard Blake
BookTrib After Dark
The Dinner Party Show
and Simon Lipskar

59871834R00086

Made in the USA
Lexington, KY
19 January 2017